Christmas

Cruise Director I

Book

C000049310

Hope Callaghan

hopecallaghan.com

Visit my website for new releases and special offers:
hopecallaghan.com

CONTENTS

CAST OF CHARACTERS III
CHAPTER 1 1
CHAPTER 2 12
CHAPTER 3 25
CHAPTER 4 38
CHAPTER 5 54
CHAPTER 6 70
CHAPTER 7 77
CHAPTER 8 91
CHAPTER 9 103
CHAPTER 10 114
CHAPTER 11 124
CHAPTER 12 139
CHAPTER 13 158
CHAPTER 14 169
CHAPTER 15 182
CHAPTER 16 197
CHAPTER 17 210
CHAPTER 18 220
CHAPTER 19 233
CHAPTER 20 246
CHAPTER 21 258
CHAPTER 22 267
CHAPTER 23 274
CHAPTER 24 285
CHAPTER 25 297
CHAPTER 26 304
CHAPTER 27 317
CHAPTER 28 327
CHAPTER 29 342
READ MORE BY HOPE 350
MEET HOPE CALLAGHAN 353
DIVINE DARK CHOCOLATE PEANUT BUTTER
BROWNIE RECIPE 354

Cast of Characters

Mildred "Millie" Sanders-Armati. Millie, heartbroken after her husband left her for one of his clients, takes a position as assistant cruise director aboard the mega cruise ship Siren of the Seas. From day one, she discovers she has a knack for solving mysteries, which is a good thing since some sort of crime is always being committed on the high seas.

Recently remarried to the ship's captain, Millie has embarked on a new adventure onboard Siren of the Seas.

Annette Delacroix. Director of Food and Beverage on board Siren of the Seas, Annette has a secret past and is the perfect accomplice in Millie's investigations. Annette is the "Jill of all Trades" and isn't afraid to roll up her sleeves and help out a friend in need.

Catherine "Cat" Wellington. Cat is the most cautious of the group of friends and prefers to help Millie from the sidelines, but when push comes to shove, Millie can count on Cat to risk life and limb in the pursuit of justice.

Danielle Kneldon. Danielle first found her way on board Siren of the Seas, working undercover. After her assignment ended, she snagged a position on board the ship and joined Millie and the gang to round out their "Super Sleuths" to a team of four.

"God made him who had no sin to be sin for us, so that in him we might become the righteousness of God." 2 Corinthians 5:21 NIV

Chapter 1

"You need to put more emotion into it," Andy said. "It's a cheerful, 'Good morning, ladies and gentlemen. This is your cruise director, Millie Armati.' Now, try it again."

"C'mon, Andy." Millie rolled her eyes. "You have your way of greeting the passengers. I have mine. What's wrong with, 'Wake up and rise to our bright morning skies. Hey, folks. This is Millie, your fun in the sun cruise director.'"

Andy gave her a thumbs down. "I suggest you stick with tradition and the standard greeting. Now give it a go."

Millie sucked in a breath and belted out, "Well...good morning, ladies and gentlemen. This is your cruise die wreck tore Millie Armati."

"Much better." Andy beamed. "I'm impressed by your attempt at incorporating a British accent, although you didn't quite pull it off."

"Maybe because I'm not British?" Millie grinned as she impulsively hugged her former boss, who was now overseeing shipboard expenses and helping train her in all things cruise director since stepping down from the prestigious position. "Are you getting nervous about the wedding?"

"Not at all. I am relieved that Cat and I decided to delay it for a couple of weeks, giving me time to get back on my feet, not to mention a chance to focus on my new position. Although I must admit, Cat seems somewhat nervous."

Millie nodded absentmindedly. Her close friend was getting cold feet and having second thoughts about marrying at this stage in her life, not to mention sharing cramped quarters. Although

Andy's "home" on board the mega cruise liner, *Siren of the Seas*, was much larger than Cat's tiny, shared cabin, it would still be a tight squeeze. Cruise ship living could be summed up in one word: compact.

The good news was both of them put in long hours, which meant they wouldn't be spending a lot of time at home.

And to be honest, Cat confided she wasn't so much nervous about marrying Andy, but was having flashbacks of her marriage to Jay Beck, an escaped convict who had kidnapped and planned to kill her.

The kidnapping was the catalyst for Cat to get the professional help she needed, and it had worked wonders. She'd put her ex and past life behind her and was embracing this new and exciting chapter, except for an occasional twinge of terror.

"She'll be fine." Millie patted his arm. "I'm sure it will be an adjustment for both of you. Remember, love conquers all. You love each other and can work out the kinks as you go along."

"I agree, Millie. If you ever grow weary of your new position as cruise director, you might consider taking up psychology. We could use a good shrink."

"No way. There are times I question my own sanity." Millie's eyes were drawn to the side of the ship and a familiar figure jogging toward the crew only exit. "Why is Danielle leaving the ship? We're supposed to be heading downstairs for one more photo shoot."

Andy craned his neck, following Millie's gaze. "She seems to be in a bit of a hurry."

"I hope everything is all right." For the past few days, Danielle had seemed somewhat jumpy, which was completely out of character for the former undercover agent who gave up a life of fighting crime to work on board their ship.

Millie secretly wondered if perhaps Danielle wasn't cut out for the added pressure of her new position as assistant cruise director.

Chalking it up to being a learning curve for both of them, she made a point of cutting her friend some slack.

"Let me send her a quick message, reminding her about our schedule." Millie tapped out a text, expecting a prompt reply, but there wasn't one. Growing concerned, she tried calling Danielle. The call went directly to voicemail. "She's not answering her cell phone."

Andy's watch app chimed. "We can't worry about Danielle. It's time to go."

Majestic Cruise Lines was officially announcing Millie as the cruise director and Danielle as the assistant cruise director.

Actually, it wasn't their *first* photo shoot, but the second. The first had been a press release, industry-wide, with the announcement of Millie's and

Danielle's upcoming promotions. Emails, notes and cards had poured in, most of them from past cruise guests who congratulated both her and Danielle.

She'd kept them all, touched by the number of people who were thrilled to hear about her promotion.

Reflecting back, it had been a long journey. The shocking discovery her husband was cheating on her with a woman she thought was a friend. Millie wanted nothing more than to curl up in bed, pull the covers over her head and wallow in self-pity.

Instead, she fought her way through those dark days, fought for a new life on her own and landed the job as assistant cruise director. Little did she know the path she blazed would include a second chance at love.

Millie led a fairytale life, and the unexpected promotion was one more exciting chapter. Not only exciting for her, but also for Danielle, who had been by her side almost from the beginning.

She cast a concerned glance in the direction her friend had gone before reluctantly following Andy down the side stairs. "I've been meaning to ask, how are you feeling?"

Andy's recent health scare had been the catalyst for him moving into the newly-created position, helping to keep the ship's costs under control.

"Thrilled to still be along for the ride." Andy placed a hand on his chest. "This old ticker needs to last long enough for me to enjoy some of my golden years."

"For a good long time."

"What about you, Millie?" Andy paused on the landing, leveling her with a thoughtful gaze. "How are you?"

"Fine. I...it's hard to explain. It feels as if I'm doing the same job I've always done, but with a little more responsibility and decision-making," Millie said. "Which can all be attributed to how well you trained me."

"I'll take that as a compliment," Andy joked.

"It was. I could not have asked for a better boss, not to mention friend."

They reached the downstairs atrium where Nic, the ship's captain, who also happened to be Millie's husband, and Donovan Sweeney, the ship's purser, stood watching for them.

Donovan waited until they drew close. "Where's Danielle?"

Andy and Millie exchanged a quick glance.

"I don't know," Millie said. "We saw her leaving the ship a short time ago. I sent her a text and tried calling, but she isn't answering."

"She's been acting a little out of sorts lately," Donovan said. "Are you sure everything is all right?"

"I hope so."

Nic glanced at his watch. "We can't wait for her."

The small group posed for several photos, answered a few questions about their new roles, and soon the fluff and fanfare was over.

"That was fun." Millie dusted her hands.

"It was delightful," Andy said. "Speaking of delightful, don't forget about our meeting with Flash and Mervin, the ventriloquist. They're the new entertainers I scheduled to join Siren of the Seas before being hospitalized."

"We've never had a ventriloquist before."

"I've been meaning to mention that Mervin has some...unusual quirks."

"The dummy or the ventriloquist?" Millie joked.

"Both. You'll see what I mean when you meet them."

"I can't wait."

The pair parted ways in front of the stairwell, with Millie making a beeline for the lower deck to see if Danielle had returned. She found Suharto, the head of gangway security, standing near the exit.

"Hello, Miss Millie, or should I say Cruise Director Armati," Suharto teased.

Millie playfully nudged him in the arm. "Very funny. I'll always be Millie to you." She quickly sobered. "I saw Danielle leaving the ship about an hour ago and she seemed to be in a hurry. Has she returned yet?"

Suharto shook his head. "I watched her leave and have been here the entire time."

"Please let me know as soon as she comes back." Millie stepped to the side and dialed Danielle's cell phone. Her stomach knotted when, once again, the call went directly to voicemail. "Danielle. It's Millie. You missed our photo shoot and I'm worried about you. Please call me back as soon as you get this message."

She ended the call and slipped past the gangway when she spotted Sharky and his scooter flying out of a building and speeding toward the ship.

Millie's heart skipped a beat when she noticed Danielle seated behind him, with her head resting on his back.

Sharky swung the scooter around. He stopped near the bottom of the gangway and hurriedly climbed off.

"Thank you." Danielle gratefully accepted the hand Sharky offered and began limping toward the ship.

Millie dashed down the gangway and abruptly stopped. "What on earth happened to you?"

Chapter 2

Millie's eyes widened in horror when she noticed the large goose egg forming on the side of Danielle's forehead. "What happened to you?" she repeated.

"I was in the cargo storage area searching for a suitcase. Next thing I know, I'm on the ground and Sharky is leaning over me." Danielle gingerly touched the bump. "And I have a whopper of a headache."

"You were flat on your back and out cold. I think you need to go to the medical center and get checked out." Sharky tapped the top of the black suitcase wedged in the scooter's front basket. "I'll hang onto this until you're done."

"Thanks, Sharky."

Millie grasped Danielle's arm and escorted her on board the ship. They scanned their keycards and turned left, making the slow trek to the medical center, where they were greeted by the nurse on duty. After a brief explanation, the women were ushered to the back, where another nurse quickly assessed Danielle's condition.

"It appears you may have suffered a concussion. Doctor Gundervan will be with you shortly."

As promised, the doctor arrived moments later. Millie excused herself, making her way to the waiting area, all the while praying for Danielle.

Ten minutes passed and then another fifteen, with no sign of her or the doctor. She sprang from her chair and started to pace.

Finally, Doctor Gundervan emerged from the back, a solemn expression on his face.

Millie rushed over. "How is Danielle?"

"She's going to be all right."

"Thank goodness." She clasped her hands, offering a silent prayer of gratitude.

"She's suffered a concussion. I'll be keeping her here for the next twenty-four hours for observation."

"Of course. I completely understand," Millie said. "I'll make sure her shift is covered."

The doctor turned to go and then paused, looking as if he wanted to say something.

"What is it?"

"I...I'm not sure if it's because of the head injury, but Danielle is giving me conflicting stories about what happened to her."

"Conflicting stories?"

"She claims she was taking a shortcut through a storage building, and then she said she went in there to search for a bag that belonged to her."

"She had a suitcase with her," Millie said. "Maybe she was doing both...cutting through the building and looking for the bag."

The doctor nodded absentmindedly. "Would you like to chat with her for a moment while I finish filling out her paperwork?"

"Yes. Thank you." Millie followed the doctor down the hall, past the examination rooms, and to a hospital room around the corner. She found a pale Danielle seated upright in bed, staring blankly into space. "Hey, bruiser."

Danielle offered her a half-hearted smile. "Bruiser is an accurate description. Literally."

Millie gingerly perched on the edge of the bed. "You're off to an exciting start as assistant cruise director," she teased. "On a more serious note, I'm glad you're going to be okay. What happened?"

"I ran over to the cargo storage building to pick up a suitcase. When I got there, I had trouble finding it."

"Maybe because there are thousands of pieces of luggage stored in the building during our turnaround days," Millie pointed out.

"No kidding, not to mention the fact I was looking for a black suitcase. Do you have any idea how many pieces of luggage are black or dark blue?" Danielle answered her own question. "Almost all of them."

"But you found it," Millie prompted.

"Finally. I was getting ready to grab it when I heard a noise. It sounded like someone running." Danielle told her she turned to see where it was coming from. "Next thing I know, I'm flat on my back, I have a splitting headache and Sharky is calling my name."

"You didn't see the person who hit you?"

"Nope."

"Crewmembers aren't randomly attacked inside the cargo storage building. They had to have been after something." Millie pressed her palms together. "At the risk of not minding my own business, what was in the suitcase?"

Danielle's eyes slid to the side. "An old friend sent it to me."

Millie arched a brow, her interest piqued. Danielle occasionally mentioned her former career as an undercover agent, followed by a brief stint as a "cop-for-hire," but she never talked about friends or family.

In fact, the only name she'd ever heard Danielle mention was her brother, Casey, who had died.

Millie waited until their eyes met. "An old friend?"

Danielle lifted her hand. "Please don't ask me, Millie. I can't...talk about it. All I can say is the suitcase is important to me."

"Important enough to take a conking on the head. Maybe I'm sticking my sleuthing hat on a little prematurely, but do you think there's a link between the suitcase and your attack?"

Her friend shook her head.

"I see. You don't want to talk about it." Millie could also see Danielle was struggling with something and that something involved the suitcase. "Hopefully, I'm way off and you were just in the wrong place at the wrong time."

"I hope you are too." Danielle clutched the edges of the sheet so tightly her knuckles turned white.

"Get some rest." Millie gave her a gentle hug, praying that whatever Danielle refused to talk about didn't involve something dangerous.

"I will."

She patted her radio. "I'm here if you need anything."

Doctor Gundervan returned, and Millie promised to stop by later to check on her.

Whatever was in the suitcase was important to Danielle. Perhaps her attack was random...or maybe not. There was only one way to find out.

*****

Before Millie could squeeze in time to track down Sharky, she needed to rearrange Danielle's schedule.

She'd often despised Andy's "zap app aka scheduling app," but now that she was in charge of the ship's entertainment schedule, Millie was quickly discovering it was a godsend for rearranging schedules and activities at the last minute.

Thankfully, she was able to cover Danielle's schedule with a few clicks of a button, and with mere minutes to spare before heading up to the lido deck to kick off the recently revamped sailaway party.

Hours earlier, Millie learned their current itinerary to the "ABC Islands" had been revised. The islands were recovering from a rare end-of-the-year storm, forcing the ports to temporarily close.

Which meant Majestic Cruise Lines had to scramble to find other ports of call. Nic had "worked his magic" and *Siren of the Seas* would now make port stops in St. Kitts, Antigua and St. Lucia, two of which Millie had never visited before.

Most of the passengers she spoke with seemed excited by the change in the schedule, to islands not in Majestic Cruise Lines' rotation. It also meant more port days once the ship reached the Leeward Islands.

Several members of the entertainment staff were on hand to help host the sailaway festivities while servers circled the deck and makeshift dance floor, offering frothy and fruity beverages to the crowd.

"You look frazzled." Millie turned to find Felix, one of the ship's dancers, standing behind her. "What happened to my perky, I'm-on-top-of-the-world cruise director?"

"Danielle is out of commission until tomorrow. She's down in medical."

Felix frowned. "Down in medical?"

"She'll be fine, but I'm treading water and could use some help."

"We're besties, Millie. What can I do?"

"I need a co-host for the Diamond Elite's Jingle Bell Ball later this evening, to help collect invitations, mix, mingle and hobnob."

"I love a good party." Felix clapped his hands. "Count me in."

Relieved to know her friend had her back, there was a spring in Millie's step as she circled the crowd. The sun was shining, and she was beginning to believe it would be smooth sailing for most of their journey.

She answered questions from several of the passengers, helped one couple access the activity app on their cell phone, and then headed down the side stairs to check in with Isla, the director of shore excursions.

"Hey, Millie." Isla greeted her with a smile. "How's it going?"

"As good as can be expected. A better question would be...how are *you*?"

Isla blew air through thinned lips. "We've been issuing excursion credits all day." She motioned to a group of excursion desk employees and the long line of passengers waiting to be helped.

"I won't keep you." Millie turned to go, and Isla stopped her. "I know you're the big cheese now and are probably crazy busy, but do you have any days off during this cruise?"

Millie consulted her schedule and found a sliver of time carved out during their port stop in St. Kitts. "I'm off the morning that we're docked in St. Kitts."

"Our first port stop," Isla said. "Lucky you."

"Why?"

"The island is awesome."

"St. Kitts. I've been trying to figure out why the name sounds familiar." Millie snapped her fingers. "Now I remember. Nic tricked me into taking a Segway tour. What's so awesome about it?"

"Brimstone Hill National Fortress. It's a UNESCO World Heritage Site."

Millie arched a brow. "I suppose it's not near the port."

"Nope, although it's an easy car ride. I've been doing some research." Isla unfolded a brochure and rattled off the highlights. "I'm going to check it out. Joy is going with me. Do you want to join us?"

"The view from the top looks amazing." Millie flipped the brochure over. "What time?"

"We're meeting at the end of the pier at nine. It's the early bird tour. There are plenty of spots still available."

Millie did a mental calculation. If she timed it right, she could be on hand for the first wave of passengers who were getting off the ship, join Isla and Joy for the tour and still be back around lunchtime. "Let me double-check my schedule. How many spots are left?"

"A bunch. I guess no one else wants to take the early morning excursion. Why?"

"I was thinking about seeing if Annette, Cat, and maybe even Danielle would like to go."

Isla tapped the keyboard. "There are several vans and tour guides showing availability. I don't see any chance of it selling out."

"Thanks, Isla. I'll let you know as soon as I can if it's a go for me or any of the others."

"You're welcome." Isla lifted her hand for a high five. "I hope you can make it. Even if it's boring, something tells me if you're along for the ride, it will still be an exciting adventure."

Millie slapped her palm. "I'll stick with a laid-back informational tour and leave the excitement to someone else."

Those words would come back to haunt her. Little did she—or Isla—know how exciting their excursion to Brimstone Hill would turn out to be.

Chapter 3

It was late afternoon before Millie had time to check on Danielle. As soon as she arrived, she could tell her friend was feeling much better.

"I can't wait to get out of here. Donovan and Captain Armati are insisting I stay here for the full twenty-four hours."

"I agree with them. Your shift is already covered. Rest and recovery are what you need. Don't worry, you can jump right back in tomorrow." Millie studied her face, noting that Danielle's color was returning. "Has Brody stopped by to see you?"

"Yeah. He surprised me with a caffeine-free mocha latte and my favorite ham and pineapple pizza. He's spoiling me rotten."

"Good. You look better. I'm going to go grab a bite to eat myself." Millie meandered toward the door, and Danielle stopped her. "While you're here, I have a favor to ask."

"Ask away."

"Can you bring me the suitcase? I'm pretty sure Sharky is still hanging onto it for me."

"Sure. I was planning on stopping by his office." Millie promised she would be back soon and then made a beeline for the head of the maintenance department's office. The lights were on, and she gave the door a tentative knock before sticking her head around the corner.

"Hey, Millie." Sharky motioned her inside. "I was just thinking about you. How's Danielle?"

"Much better. Gundervan is keeping her overnight for observation." Millie eased the door shut behind her. "What exactly happened earlier?"

"I was checking in a delivery of fruit and noticed Danielle hurrying into the cargo storage building. I didn't think too much about it since the crew uses it as a shortcut to avoid the bottleneck in the passenger terminal."

"I've used it a time or two," Millie said. "You know what a madhouse the terminal is on turnaround day."

"Right? So, I finished inspecting the bananas and was meeting with the ship chandler, our liaison for provisions, when I heard someone scream." Sharky told Millie he thought it was coming from the cargo storage building. "When I got inside, I'm pretty sure I saw someone running out the door. I started heading that way when I noticed Danielle on the floor."

"Were you able to get a look at the person?"

Sharky shook his head.

"And no other crewmembers were around?"

"Nope. Once the luggage and other stuff are turned over to the porters, they bring it into the building and no one is allowed to move the bags until the drug-sniffing dogs do their thing. We were still waiting for them."

"Interesting," Millie murmured.

Fin, Sharky's cat, stalked over and began nudging her hand. "Hey, buddy." She scratched his ears. "You're looking a little chunky these days. Sharky must be feeding you good."

"I found this new brand of sardines." Sharky motioned to a tall stack of canned sardines crammed on top of his filing cabinet. "Fin loves them and can't seem to get enough. There's only one problem."

Fin rubbed up against Millie's arm, purring loudly. He opened his mouth and a foul stench blasted out.

Millie's hand flew to her face. She made a gagging sound. "That's gross."

"Fin has some stinky burps." Sharky chuckled. "I should have warned you, seeing how he just polished off a can."

"What an awful smell."

"If he didn't love them so much, I would try to get him to eat something else."

"Scout's favorite treats smell nasty, so I completely understand." Millie fanned her face. "Back to Danielle's attack. Where did you find her? Near the front, the back, the overhead doors?"

"I can show you the exact spot." Sharky shifted his laptop and reached for his mouse. "This is a layout of the cargo area. I use it to keep track of everything that's loaded and unloaded."

Millie slipped her reading glasses on. "The passenger luggage loading and unloading area is on the left."

"And I found Danielle right about here." Sharky tapped the screen. "I'm sorry I don't have anything else to go on. Patterson was down here earlier asking questions. I told him the same thing I told you. Do you know if Danielle saw anyone?"

"Nope. She said she thought she heard someone coming up behind her. The next thing she remembers is you staring down at her." Millie slowly stood. "The reason I'm here is she asked if I could bring the suitcase to her."

"I locked it up over in the holding area." Sharky shoved his chair back. "I'll go get it."

While Sharky left to grab the suitcase, Millie meandered over to his bookcase and began studying his framed photos. One in particular caught her eye. It was Sharky, clad in swim trunks and a t-shirt, with a snorkeling mask strapped to his forehead. He stood next to a gray-haired woman who was holding a metal detector in one hand and what appeared to be a handful of rocks in the other.

Sharky returned, dragging a black suitcase behind him. "This is it. I don't know what's in here, but it's pretty light."

"I don't know either." Millie tapped the side of the picture frame. "Have you heard from Elvira lately?"

"Yeah. We have something in the works."

"In the works?" Millie lifted a brow.

"She invited me to Savannah, Georgia. I'm her date for Carlita Garlucci's wedding."

"That's right. Carlita is marrying soon. I have a wedding gift for her. Maybe you can take it up there for me."

"Sure. Bring it by whenever you have a chance." Sharky eased the suitcase against the wall and joined Millie near the bookcase. "Elvira and I were treasure hunting. We look good together, huh?"

"You seem well-suited," Millie said diplomatically.

Fin, who was cleaning himself, scrambled to his feet. He arched his back in a long stretch. Curious to check out the suitcase Sharky had brought in, he stalked across the floor and sniffed the corner.

Yeowl. Fin let out an ear-piercing yowl and began pawing the handle.

Goosebumps ran down Millie's arms, not because of Fin's yowl, but because of what it meant. The cat had keen senses, so keen he could track down missing pets, namely Scout. He was also an expert at sniffing out drugs.

Sharky voiced what Millie was already thinking. "There's something up with Danielle's suitcase."

"Fin is trying to tell us something's inside."

"You know what this means." Sharky reached for his cell phone and tapped the screen. "Hey, Patterson. Sharky here. Remember the suitcase I was hanging onto for Danielle? Fin's alerting me that there's something inside. I'll wait until you get here to open it."

Sharky ended the call and waved his phone in the air. "Patterson is on his way."

Long, tense moments passed as Fin continued yowling. Meanwhile, Millie paced and Sharky rummaged around in his drawer.

He pulled out a box of rubber gloves and tossed a pair to her. "You're gonna need these."

"For what?"

"Inspecting the contents of Danielle's suitcase, to avoid contaminating potential evidence."

"You're right." A sick feeling settled in the pit of Millie's stomach as she slipped the gloves on.

Heavy footsteps echoed in the outer corridor. Dave Patterson, the ship's head of security, appeared. He gave Millie a curt nod and turned to Sharky. "Where is it?"

Fin let out another yowl as he stood guarding the suitcase.

"He's been yowling at it ever since I brought it in here."

Patterson reached inside his pocket, pulled out his own set of gloves, and slipped them on.

"Those are nice." Sharky admired the deluxe, thick blue gloves. "They're a lot nicer than my cheapies. Like they fit snugly, but not too tight. I have fat fingers and am always struggling to get my gloves on. Where did you get them, if you don't mind me asking?"

"From my office." Patterson tugged a second set from his pocket and tossed them to Sharky. "Here, you can have my extra pair."

"Thanks." Sharky slid them on. "You wanna do the honors, or should I?"

"I'll open it. You might need to relocate Fin." Patterson motioned to the cat who was giving him the stink eye. "He's a good guard cat. Maybe a little too good."

"We've been working on training." Sharky scooped him up. "I read somewhere that cats can't be trained, but this one can. Of course, Fin is special, so I'm not surprised."

"Let's see what he found." Patterson hoisted the suitcase. "It doesn't weigh much. Has Danielle mentioned what's inside?"

"No," Sharky and Millie said in unison.

"She told me a friend sent it to her," Millie added.

Sharky cleared a spot on his desk. "You can put it right here."

Millie held her breath, watching as the head of security placed the suitcase on top. He unzipped both ends and lifted the cover.

In one section was a book of music, with handwritten notes jotted on the cover. There was also a zippered baggie with pictures inside.

Millie peeked over Patterson's shoulder and noticed a photo of a young man with blond hair. He was thin, almost too thin, and something about his expression caught her eye. "This guy looks stoned."

The way he was standing, at an odd angle. The half-closed eyes, lopsided grin, gazing at the camera as if in a daze.

"I think I know who this is," she said. "It's Danielle's brother, Casey."

"Let's see what's on the other side." Patterson carefully set the items on the desk and unzipped the second compartment. He removed a handful of grocery bags and placed them alongside the photos and music book.

"It's empty," Millie said. "Why would someone send Danielle an almost empty suitcase?"

"Maybe not." Patterson ran a gloved hand along the frame and then the sides. "I need a knife."

"I have one." Sharky pulled a pocketknife from his pants pocket and handed it to him.

"Thank you." He flipped it open and cut a clean line along the side of the suitcase. He pulled out another plastic grocery bag and this time Millie could see there was something in it.

She watched as he untied the top and removed a smaller dark brown bag.

Patterson shifted slightly, giving Millie an unobstructed view of what he was doing. She began to feel lightheaded. "It can't be," she whispered under her breath.

Chapter 4

"Drugs." Millie blurted out the first thing that popped into her head.

"It appears to be the case." Patterson's jaw tightened as he continued unwrapping the white brick. "Are you positive this suitcase belongs to Danielle?"

Millie struggled to remember exactly what Danielle had said. "Sharky?"

"Yeah. I mean, this was the suitcase she was in the cargo storage area looking for."

"Did she check the contents?" the head of security asked.

"No. She was out cold when I found her. I had to help her up and onto the scooter. I crammed the suitcase into my scooter's basket and we came straight back to the ship."

Millie picked up. "I was there when they got to the gangway. Sharky took the suitcase while I accompanied Danielle to medical."

Patterson finished his inspection. He placed the block of powder back inside, and zipped the bag shut. After finishing, he examined the exterior, searching for identification. "I see Danielle's name and the port address printed on the front, but there's no return address."

"She mentioned she had trouble finding it. There's a green and white tie-dyed cloth wrapped around the handle," Millie pointed out.

"It makes no sense," Patterson said. "Why would she pick up a suitcase with no return address?"

"But it had her name on the front," Millie said. "My thought is, if Danielle had any inkling about what was inside, there's no way she would let Sharky hang onto it for her. She knows. We all know Fin has a nose for sniffing out drugs."

"Something isn't adding up," Sharky chimed in.

"I'll chat with Danielle as soon as I confirm exactly what it is we have on our hands." He motioned to the head of maintenance. "What about the dogs? They didn't pick up on this when it was down in the port's cargo storage area?"

"We were still waiting for them when I found Danielle."

"So, the luggage and personal items being brought on board for the new voyage were in the hold, waiting for the dogs. Danielle went in there to grab the suitcase and someone attacked her."

"Looking back, I should've left it in the storage area and not brought it on board the ship. I was more concerned about Danielle than following procedure."

"Yes, you should have. Mistakes happen. Unfortunately, this could be a very big one." Patterson pinned him with a stare.

"Sorry, boss." Sharky's shoulders slumped. "I guess I screwed up."

Patterson set the suitcase on the floor and wheeled it toward the door with Millie hurrying after him. "Do you mind if I tag along for verification and your conversation with Danielle?"

"I would be surprised if you didn't want to. Let's get this over with."

"I'm here if you need me for anything else." Sharky caught Millie's eye on the way out, giving her a look that said it all. If Danielle was involved in a drug trafficking scheme, not only would Majestic Cruise Lines fire her, but she would also be locked up in the ship's jail until the authorities arrived to pick her up.

Millie was no expert concerning illegal drugs, but if she had to guess, the brick Patterson had found inside the suitcase was enough to put her friend behind bars for a very long time.

She quietly mulled over the current turn of events, falling into step with Patterson as they made their way to his office at the other end of the corridor.

Danielle was well-liked and well-respected by both the staff and crewmembers. As far as she knew, there had never been a single whisper or even a hint of her involvement in illegal or illicit activity.

"Remember, innocent until proven guilty," Millie said. "Danielle has never been involved in any sort of behavior that warranted being reprimanded, written up or investigated."

"You're joking." Patterson cleared his throat as he unlocked his office door. "I can give multiple examples of instances when Danielle has been reprimanded and, as luck would have it, *you* were also involved."

"But we're the good guys," Millie argued. "We've both been instrumental in helping solve crimes and tracking down the bad guys."

"I'm not disagreeing but merely pointing out your statement about her never being reprimanded is inaccurate."

"You know what I mean." Millie followed Patterson inside, her stomach churning as she watched the head of security place the suitcase on top of his desk. Still wearing the rubber gloves, he adjusted his grip before unzipping it. He lifted the lid and removed the white brick.

"It sure looks like drugs," Millie sighed.

"It does." Patterson removed a small test kit from the nearby locked cabinet and set it alongside the contents in question. Using the pointed end of a knife, he carved out a small sample and carefully set it on top of a glass slide.

Millie inched closer, watching as he opened a silver packet. Inside was a single cotton swab.

Her heart pounded loudly as he dipped the swab in the powder, rolling it back and forth several times. After finishing, he pressed it against a strip of paper.

Although it seemed like an eternity, it was only a matter of seconds before he lifted the swab, his expression growing even grimmer. The test strip and cotton swab were both bright blue.

"It tested positive, didn't it?" Millie's voice was barely above a whisper.

"Yes. Positive for cocaine." Patterson dropped the swab on top of the paper, grabbed his cell phone, and snapped a picture. He took a picture of the results, the block of cocaine, the wrapper, the suitcase—front, back, inside and out and then began placing the contents back inside.

"What are you going to do? We aren't one hundred percent certain the suitcase belongs to Danielle. She may have grabbed the wrong one."

"Except for the fact her name and the port address are clearly printed on the shipping label."

"But why was she attacked?"

"Because someone knew about the suitcase and contents."

"I don't have all the answers." Millie bit her lower lip. "But something isn't adding up. There's no way Danielle went into the storage building to pick up a suitcase of cocaine. I think she was set up."

"You're getting ahead of yourself," Patterson warned. "I need Danielle to confirm the bag was hers, label or not."

Millie sucked in a breath, certain it was all a terrible misunderstanding. The bag belonged to someone else. It was mislabeled and Danielle had inadvertently grabbed the wrong one.

Patterson set it on the floor and began wheeling it toward the door.

"Are you taking it to her now to see what she has to say?"

"I am."

Millie followed him into the corridor. "I'm going with you."

"I know you care about Danielle, but there's nothing you can do to help her. The bag either belongs to her or it doesn't."

"As her boss, I have a right to be there while you question her," Millie argued.

Patterson strode to the other end of the corridor, passing by several crewmembers on their way. He didn't slow, didn't change his pace. In other words, he was a man on a mission.

They reached the medical center and stepped inside.

"Hello," Patterson greeted the woman behind the desk. "Is Doctor Gundervan available?"

"He's in his office." She popped out of the chair, glancing at Patterson's nametag and then hurried into the back.

Moments later, the ship's doctor appeared. "Hello, Dave."

"Good afternoon, Joe. Do you still have Danielle Kneldon under your care?"

"I do."

"How is she?"

"She's suffered a mild traumatic brain injury."

"Brain injury," Millie gasped.

"The technical term for a concussion," the doctor explained. "The key word being mild. I expect Danielle will make a full recovery. She's eager to get out of here and has been asking if Millie has returned with her suitcase."

"She's looking for this." Patterson, still wearing the same rubber gloves, patted the handle.

"I..." The doctor stared at the gloves, and Millie could only imagine what was running through his head. "I see."

"Do you think she's up to chatting with me, chatting with us?" Patterson asked.

"She's fully alert and isn't having any issues with speech, memory or range of motion, so I would say she is."

"Would you mind checking with her? Let her know we have her suitcase."

"I will." The doctor cast one more puzzled glance at Patterson and the gloves and disappeared in the back.

He returned moments later. "She's awake and waiting for you." The doctor led Patterson down the hall to Danielle's room.

Millie trailed behind, her mind whirling. Danielle was going to be blindsided and there wasn't a single thing she could do about it other than stand by and watch it happen.

But Danielle was strong. She had a law enforcement background and could hold her own. Patterson would see. She would have a perfectly good explanation. Surely, the suitcase wasn't hers. It couldn't be.

They found Danielle seated upright in bed, her hands folded in front of her. Her eyes lit when she saw Patterson wheeling the bag into the room.

It quickly faded when she noticed his gloves. "What's going on?"

Patterson answered her question with one of his own. "Hello, Danielle. How are you feeling?"

"Like I got hit by a dump truck. Other than that, I'm dandy."

"Doctor Gundervan said he expects you'll make a full recovery."

"I'll leave you now." The doctor hurriedly backed out of the room, and Millie could hear the door close at the end of the hall.

"Millie?" Danielle's eyes darted to hers. "Why is Patterson looking at me like he does when we get busted sneaking into a passenger's cabin?"

"I..." Millie briefly closed her eyes and shook her head. "I'm sorry, Danielle."

He set the suitcase on the tray table and wheeled it around to the side. "I know we chatted about your attack earlier, but I would like you to tell me again what happened."

Danielle repeated the story, how an old friend had sent her something. She went to the cargo storage building to pick it up. "I had trouble finding it, but finally did. I heard a noise and turned around to see where it was coming from. The next thing I know, I'm flat on my back with a splitting headache and Sharky is staring down at me."

"You can confirm this is the suitcase you went to pick up." Patterson placed a gloved hand on top of it.

"It is. I have no idea why you're wearing gloves, but it can't be good."

"A label with your name and the port address is on the front, but there's no return address," he said. "Are you certain this is the suitcase you were supposed to pick up?"

"Yes."

"You don't think the labels could've been mixed up?" Patterson pressed.

"No. The sender told me they were tying a green and white tie-dyed rag around the handle."

"Where did this suitcase come from?"

"A friend sent me some personal items with sentimental value." Danielle lifted her chin, defiantly meeting the gaze of the head of security. "You had no right to search it."

Patterson slowly circled the bed, kneeling down until he was eye level with her. "This is very important, Danielle. What sentimental personal items were you expecting?"

Her jaw tightened. "Stuff. Pictures. A music book belonging to..." Her voice cracked, and she lowered her head, unable to continue.

Millie could feel tears burn the back of her eyes and her suspicions about who the young man in the photograph was and exactly how important and precious the items inside the suitcase were to Danielle were confirmed.

Patterson cast Millie a puzzled look and motioned for her to take his place.

"You were picking up things that belonged to your brother, Casey," she said in a soft voice as she took Danielle's hand.

"His friend, Emilio. He was moving to the islands and cleaning out a storage unit he and Casey shared. He said he found some personal things and wanted to know if I wanted them. I wired him some cash, and he promised to send the stuff. He lied, didn't he?"

"There are some personal items in the suitcase," Millie said. "There's also something else."

"Something else?" Danielle's head shot up, her tear-filled eyes meeting Millie's. "Drugs."

Patterson shifted his feet. "Cocaine. How did you know?"

"Emilio was...is a drug addict. So was my brother. He died of a drug overdose a little over a year before I joined Siren of the Seas. It was all my fault."

"You've said that before," Millie said in a low voice. "I know you didn't kill your brother, so how did he die?"

"I didn't think... So many times, I've wished I could go back to that day and do things differently." Danielle closed her eyes, sucked in a breath and relived the day that had haunted her, had caused her so much heartache and so many years of regret.

Chapter 5

"Hey, worrywart. You know I'm clean." Casey playfully punched his sister in the arm. "Like I told you, I'm gonna grab some things I left at Emilio's, hang out with a few of my buddies, and will be ready to come home by the time you finish your errands."

"You're sure you wanna do this? You won't be tempted?" Danielle asked. "I don't mind going with you. We'll grab your things and you can run errands with me. I'll even spring for one of those fancy latte frothy whipped drinks you've been jonesing for."

"Nah." Casey waved dismissively, his face beaming. "I've got this. Seriously. I need to be able to trust myself. I've been clean for months now. In fact, I'm hoping Emilio will see how much I've changed and consider cleaning up his act."

Danielle hesitated. It was true. Casey *had* gone off the drugs after overdosing and nearly dying. A few months in the rehab center Danielle had paid for had done wonders.

Casey was clean. He was sober. He was looking forward to his future, maybe even finding a girlfriend and settling down. All positive moves in the right direction, much to Danielle's relief after years of having him fall off the wagon and then climb back on.

Danielle and Casey's parents were out of the picture with little to no family other than each other. And Danielle, being the big sister, felt responsible for him. He'd gotten mixed up with the wrong crowd as a teen and now, years later, they were still fighting the demons that made Casey choose drugs.

"Call me if you become uncomfortable or if you need me to come back and pick you up before I'm done." She patted her pocket. "I'll be less than half an hour away."

"Will do." Casey sprang from the passenger seat. "I'm cool. It's all good." He started to close the door and swung it back open. "Thanks, Danielle."

"For what?"

"For never giving up on me. You're the best sister a brother could ask for."

Danielle's throat clogged. "You're welcome. I love you. I know how good life can be if you give it a chance."

"I'm going to. This is my shot and I know I can do this. Love you, Sis." Casey made a fist and thumped his chest. "See you soon."

"Hey!"

Casey slammed the door, drowning out Danielle's voice.

She watched as he sprinted down the sidewalk and disappeared inside the dilapidated apartment building on Chicago's south side.

Danielle shifted into park and shut the car off. She reached for the door handle and paused as an internal battle waged. On the one hand, she had a valid reason to be concerned about Casey "hanging out" with his old druggie friend, Emilio.

On the other, she couldn't follow Casey around for the rest of his life. He needed to prove to himself he could resist the temptation of falling back into his old life, his old habits.

Danielle sat staring at the building for several long moments, praying Casey would have the strength to resist the temptations that had almost taken his life before starting her car and slowly driving off.

She rushed through her errands, stopping at the bank to transfer money into a joint checking account with her brother so he would have bus fare for the new job he was starting at the oil change shop a few blocks from home. Checking her post office box was next, followed by a trip to the local store to grab some extra groceries. When clean and sober, Casey was an eating machine.

Her last stop was the local coffee shop, where she grabbed her favorite latte and one for her brother.

Danielle drove back to Emilio's apartment building and eased into an empty parking spot. She checked to make sure her car doors were locked before texting Casey to let him know she was out front.

Danielle sipped her coffee and waited, watching as two men casually strolled to the corner. They huddled together, and she noticed them swapping something. *Drugs.*

Casting an anxious glance toward Emilio's upper-level living room window, Danielle checked her phone. There was no word from Casey.

She waited another ten minutes, her anxiety increasing. Danielle dialed her brother's cell phone.

The call went directly to voicemail. "Casey. It's me. I'm at Emilio's waiting for you."

Danielle checked her watch. Almost half an hour had passed—a half an hour past their agreed upon time. She unclasped her purse and ran a light hand across the cool metal of her concealed weapon.

With a quick check of her surroundings, Danielle exited her vehicle, hurried around the front and jogged to the door. She rang Emilio's doorbell and waited.

A heat crept up the back of her neck. She warily turned and noticed the two men who had completed their "transaction" on the street corner were now standing at the end of the sidewalk watching her.

Warning bells went off in Danielle's head. Her training and instinct told her she was being sized up. Any minute now, the two men would confront her, curious to find out who she was and what she was doing.

Gritting her teeth, Danielle jabbed the bell again. Still no answer.

Out of the corner of her eye, she watched as the men did exactly what she anticipated and meandered toward her.

Trapped and with nowhere to go, she spun around while simultaneously reaching inside her purse and wrapping her hand around her handgun. "Hello," she coolly greeted them.

"Hey." One of the men, clad in torn jeans, a denim jacket and sporting a scruffy beard, nodded casually. "You lookin' for someone?"

"Emilio."

"He ain't here," the second man said. "He left about an hour ago."

"Was he with a blond-haired guy?"

"Yeah. Casey. He was with Casey. You know them?" the bearded man asked.

"I was supposed to pick Casey up."

"They won't be back for a while," the second man said. "They had some business they were going to take care of."

"What kind of business?"

Shaggy laughed. "What are you, the po-po?"

"Casey's my brother." Danielle tightened her grip on the gun as one of them inched closer. "Do you know where I can find them?"

"On the streets. Anywhere on the streets," Shaggy said.

Danielle's cell phone rang. She quickly glanced at the screen, her heart plummeting. A "spam likely" call. Not Casey. She quickly sidestepped the men, mumbling under her breath, and made a hasty retreat. She didn't stop until she reached her car.

Danielle climbed inside, locked the doors, and grabbed her cell phone. Casey had finally texted her back.

Hey, Sis. Emilio asked me to hang with him. He's going to drop me off at your place later. Don't wait up. He signed it "C" and added a peace sign meme.

She promptly called him. As suspected, it went right to voicemail. Casey avoiding her calls meant only one thing. Her brother was on his way back to the dark side.

*****

Danielle drove up and down Chicago's south side streets, slowing every time she saw anyone even slightly resembling her brother or Emilio. In between, Danielle kept texting, begging her brother to let her know where to find him.

But each attempt was met with silence. Complete and total silence.

Dusk set in and Danielle was getting more and more stares. More and more looks from the locals. She decided to circle one more block, one she'd heard Casey mention before, and thought she may have spotted him.

Without warning, a wild-eyed, heavily tattooed man appeared out of nowhere. He flung himself on the hood of her car and began pounding on her windshield.

Danielle slammed on the brakes. The crazed man slid off and began cussing her out. Despite her training and background, even a seasoned police officer wouldn't be caught dead in the area alone and at night, let alone a woman.

With nothing left to do, she drove back to her apartment, grabbed her groceries, and trudged up the stairs. Danielle clung to a glimmer of hope Casey had found his way back to her place. But her apartment was empty.

Nothing had been touched. Casey had not been there and the sinking feeling in the pit of her stomach told her he wasn't coming back, at least not tonight.

Danielle fixed a frozen dinner for one, keeping her cell phone by her side in the off chance Casey called. But there was no call.

She barely slept that night, having a vivid dream about a trip the siblings had taken, camping at Lake Mirror. The backdrop of the mountains glimmered across the deep blue waters of the lake.

"Hey, knucklehead. I thought you were picking wild berries for the pie you promised to make me."

Danielle spun around and found Casey grinning at her. He playfully nudged his sister, his eyes full of mischief.

"I was on my way," she said as she nodded at the small fishing boat propped up against a boulder, tucked in behind a thick clump of grass. "Maybe after I finish picking berries, we can go fishing."

"Right after you make my pie." Casey wiped droplets of sweat from his brow. "I don't know about you, but a swim in the lake sounds good. This heat is brutal. Race you to the water." He didn't wait for a reply and ran off.

"Casey! That's not fair!" Danielle sprinted across the field of wildflowers in hot pursuit of her brother, but Casey easily reached the water's edge first.

He sifted through the stones and picked one up, studying it as he ran his thumb over the smooth surface.

"Check this out." Casey flicked his wrist and sent the stone skimming across the tranquil waters.

"You still haven't taught me how to do that," Danielle scolded when she got close.

"Because you're a slow learner," he teased and then bent down to find another stone. He picked it up and studied it. "This'll do. Now pay attention this time."

He demonstrated his stone-skipping technique. Eager to try her hand, Danielle began sifting through the stones, searching for the perfect one.

She ran the tip of her sandal over a small pile and spied one that looked promising.

"Not that one." Casey snatched it from her hand. "This one is special. This side is the color of your eyes." He flipped it over. "And this side is the color of mine. See?"

He was right. Each side of the rock was a different shade—one side a lighter blue and the other a deeper hue.

"You need to keep it. It will bring you luck. Plus, whenever you look at it, it will remind you of me," he told her.

"You're right." Danielle nodded as she rubbed the small stone. "I'll keep it forever." She slipped it in her pocket and reached for another one.

"I have a surprise for you," Casey told her before he spun around and jogged along the edge of the lake. "I'll be right back."

Danielle's heart began to race, and a wave of fear washed over her. Warning bells went off in her head. Something bad was about to happen.

She reached out to grab Casey's arm. "Don't go!"

It was too late. Her brother had already circled around the edge of the lake, headed toward their cabin on the other side.

Danielle chased after him. "Wait!" She watched in horror as her brother faltered. He swayed for a moment and then fell to the ground.

"No! Casey!" Danielle raced along the water's edge, her entire body, her mind focused on one thing…reaching her brother. But it was as if she was moving in slow motion. The faster she ran, the slower she moved.

She finally reached Casey and found him lying face down.

Danielle dropped to her knees. She gently turned him over. A small trickle of blood trailed along his cheek and she began to feel lightheaded. "No…"

Danielle bolted upright in bed, struggling to catch her breath, her eyes darting around the dark bedroom. "A dream. It was only a dream."

She found it impossible to go back to sleep, the feeling something terrible had happened to her brother lingering in the back of her mind. Finally, early the next morning, she crawled out of bed and shuffled to the kitchen to start a pot of coffee.

Danielle headed back to the bedroom and grabbed her cell phone off the charger. She carried it into the kitchen and set it on the counter. The vivid dream lingered in her mind. What had started out as a sweet dream had turned into her worst nightmare.

After coffee and a shower, Danielle returned to the kitchen. Her heart skipped a beat when she discovered she'd missed a call. Not from Casey, but from an unknown number. Whoever it was had left a message.

Danielle entered her password and hit the speaker button. "Hey, Danielle. It's Emilio. We got a bad gram. I told Casey we should've passed, but it was cheap. Man, I'm sorry. He went fast."

She fought off the urge to throw up and dialed Emilio's number. "Emilio. It's Danielle. What's going on?"

"I'm sorry." Emilio began rambling, and she cut him off. "Where's Casey?"

"Gone."

"Gone where?"

"It was a bad trip." Emilio began rambling again, and it quickly became clear Danielle's nightmare was a premonition of what was to come. Her brother was dead.

Chapter 6

Danielle's voice remained flat as she relived the moment she learned about her brother's death. "He and Emilio got their hands on some bad cocaine."

"What about your parents?" Millie asked. "I'm not sure if you've ever mentioned them."

"They were dead to me and Casey. As in, they weren't there for us. I practically raised my brother. I'm sure they're out there somewhere, but as far as we were concerned, we were pretty much on our own."

Millie wrapped both arms around her and gave her a gentle hug. "You can't blame yourself for his death. You were trying to help and didn't know what was going to happen after he got out of your car."

"Casey was doing so good. I should have gone up there with him to pick up his stuff. Instead, I left."

"I'm sorry, Danielle, for your loss," Patterson said. "Is Casey the reason you went into law enforcement?"

"Yep. To get drugs off the streets." Danielle laughed bitterly. "It didn't help my brother, did it?"

"That's a lot to bottle up," Millie said. "And wrongly carry around. You did not kill your brother."

Danielle sucked in a breath. "Emilio was always a wheeler-dealer, trying to break into the big leagues. My guess is he shipped me a bunch of drugs, thinking I would unknowingly bring them on board for him. The plan is for us to meet in St. Kitts. I return his suitcase. He gets his cocaine."

"It's beginning to look that way," Patterson said.

"Can I see what else is inside?"

Patterson unzipped the suitcase, removed the music book and photos, and held them up. "Unfortunately, I can't let you have them. They're potential evidence." He tapped the top of the cocaine. "This was also inside, sewed into the lining."

"That's why you mentioned you might need time off in St. Kitts...to meet Emilio," Millie said.

"Yeah. He said he had something else belonging to Casey but kept insisting he wanted to give it to me in person."

"Didn't you find it odd that he didn't just plan to meet you in St. Kitts with all your brother's belongings?" Patterson asked.

"You know druggies don't always do things that make sense," Danielle said. "Besides, I wanted to take what I could get before Emilio changed his mind."

"True."

Her eyes flashed with anger. "He must think I'm an idiot."

"Not an idiot," Patterson disagreed. "But maybe someone desperate to get what little you had left of your brother back."

"He told me he was only moving with one suitcase and it was already full. That's when he came up with the idea of me sending cash and him forwarding some of Casey's things. My gut told me not to trust him. I went against my better judgment."

Millie motioned to Patterson. "We should check the passenger manifest to see if he's onboard."

"I was already planning to. What's Emilio's last name?"

"Torres."

"Emilio Torres," Patterson repeated. "Is there anything else you can think of?"

"No." Danielle lifted her head. "I'm surprised there was anything left and Emilio didn't try selling the stuff for money, although I can't imagine anyone paying for some old photos and a music book."

"I'll need to report the drugs," Patterson said. "The good news is it will take time to put a report together and submit it back in the States."

Danielle's shoulders slumped. "I know the drill. As of right now, I'm on the hook for this."

"Unless you follow through with your plan to meet Emilio, we inform the authorities of the goods transfer and they arrest him in St. Kitts," Patterson said.

"What if Emilio doesn't know anything about the drugs?"

"Danielle," Millie chided. "What are the odds of that?"

Danielle formed a "zero" with her thumb and index finger. "Nada. Zip."

"You don't owe Emilio anything. He's using you to transport an illegal substance to a foreign country. You, more than anyone, should know this is not only dangerous, but it will guarantee you a long prison sentence if you were to get caught."

"True. I don't want to believe it, but the bottom line is he's using me." Danielle placed a light hand on her forehead.

"How did he know how to find you?" Patterson asked.

"Emilio knew I worked on board the cruise ship. He must've tracked me down, figured out where we were going, and came up with a brilliant plan to get his drugs to his new home," Danielle said. "As I mentioned before, he was the wheeler-dealer of the bunch."

"So, whoever conked you on the head was also looking for the suitcase," Patterson theorized. "Sharky showed up and scared them off before they could grab it and now someone is going to be on the hunt for those drugs."

"You know it." Danielle winced. "I guess I had better get to feeling one hundred percent better if the goal is for me to be involved in an international drug trafficking sting."

"I'll be requesting a copy of the surveillance camera recordings in and around the cargo storage building." Patterson offered her a grim smile. "We have no choice but to locate your brother's friend."

"He gave me a cell phone number and said he would contact me as soon as we arrived in St. Kitts Tuesday morning."

"I don't like the idea of Danielle going alone." Millie thought about her earlier conversation with Isla, how there were spots available on the early morning island excursion. "You need to be able to control the situation, and I think I have the perfect spot where you can meet Emilio."

Chapter 7

"No one is going anywhere or doing anything without a proper plan in place," Patterson said sternly. "We need to make sure Danielle is up to leaving the ship. Secondly, we'll be in a foreign country."

"We won't be doing anything illegal," Millie pointed out. "Danielle delivers the suitcase minus the drugs. We get a confession. You nail Emilio and then..." Her voice trailed off.

Patterson folded his arms. "And then what? We kidnap him and bring him onboard the ship? This could be tricky. We'll have to get the local authorities involved. We're also working with a big 'if,' in proving Emilio was the one who put the cocaine in the suitcase."

"Can't we just toss it over the side of the ship and pretend it never happened?" Danielle joked. "I mean, it's a win-win. We get it off the streets. I'm off the hook and no one gets hurt."

"I'm sure more than one load of illegal drugs is sitting at the bottom of the ocean," Patterson said. "But that's not the solution. We may have to give this a little thought."

"Brimstone Hill," Millie said. "It's in somewhat of an out-of-the-way area, at least that's the impression I got. If Danielle and Emilio meet early in the morning, there won't be many people around. You'll be able to isolate him and reduce the risk of loss."

"Listen to you. Sounding all strategic," Patterson sighed. "Our first step is to set up a meeting. If the man is involved, he's going to want those drugs back."

Millie's watch app chimed. It was a message from Andy. "I have to run. I'm meeting with a ventriloquist Andy hired before he became ill."

After promising to check on Danielle first thing the following morning, Millie headed out. She passed by the crew's dining room and her stomach grumbled, reminding her it had been a long time since her last meal.

She stepped inside, her heart plummeting when she saw the buffet's long line. Figuring she would have better luck finding food somewhere else, Millie made a mad dash to the galley where she found her close friend, Annette Delacroix, holding a staff meeting.

Millie slipped off to the side and began sifting through the RTG—ready-to-go sack meals. Although the selection was limited, the roast beef on rye looked tasty.

She found a quiet spot near the dessert prep area in the back. Removing the sandwich from the wrapper, she slathered on a thick layer of horseradish sauce and took a big bite.

"Miss Millie."

She turned to find Amit, Annette's right-hand man, standing behind her. "Where have you been hiding? I have not seen you all day."

"It's been crazy busy." Millie held up the sandwich before taking another bite. "I've been dealing with one crisis right after another."

"A typical day in the life of a cruise director," Amit teased.

"You know it." Millie pointed to an array of decadent brownies. "What are those luscious-looking treats?"

"My dark chocolate brownies," Amit said. "They're a new dessert we are selling in Celebrations. You will see them at tonight's Diamond Elite Jingle Bell Ball."

"I love dark chocolate," she hinted.

"You must try one. Although I have to warn you they are very rich."

"Meaning a small piece goes a long way."

"Correct." Amit slid a fork under one of the brownies and eased it onto a small plate. "Tell me what you think."

"I'm a bit of a brownie aficionado," she jokingly boasted. "It's going to have to be pretty awesome."

"It is," Amit said confidently. "I have mastered the recipe."

Millie's mouth watered as she inspected the layered treat. "I love peanut butter. I love dark chocolate and walnuts are divine." She nibbled the corner, savoring the rich chocolate, mingled with the creamy peanut butter.

"Well?"

"You should call them Amit's divine dark chocolate peanut butter brownies." Millie polished off the piece. "The guests are going to love them."

"I hope so. I am always looking for new desserts."

"This one ticks all the boxes." Millie reached into the ready-to-go meal bag and removed a container of celery sticks. "And now a little something healthy to wash it all down."

Annette strolled across the galley. "Hey, stranger. How are things in the entertainment world?"

"Busy. No wonder poor Andy needed a break. This job isn't for the faint of heart."

"I heard you're on top of your game. New shows, new lineup, fabulous holiday entertainment." Annette placed a hand on her hip. "I also heard Danielle is down in medical. Someone attacked her in the cargo storage building. I hope they found the person."

"There's a little more to the story." Millie briefly filled her friends in on Danielle's contact with Emilio, leaving out the part about how he was directly linked to her brother Casey's death. "From what we can piece together, he set Danielle up by returning some of her brother's things with plans for her to transport the drugs to St. Kitts."

"But you're not one hundred percent certain," Annette said.

"Nope. We'll have to wait to see what Emilio has to say when he contacts Danielle." Millie shared her thoughts. "If that's the case, Isla has some spots available for the St. Kitts / Brimstone Hill early morning excursion. We could tag along with Danielle while Patterson and the authorities wait at the top for the exchange and then..."

"Bam." Annette smacked her palms together. "The drug dealer, along with what sounds like a significant amount of cocaine, is off the streets."

"Patterson hasn't committed yet, but I think he's considering it," Millie said.

"What time?" Annette snagged the clipboard off the wall and flipped the page. "I'm working Tuesday morning."

"I can cover for you, Miss Annette," Amit offered. "Most passengers will get off the ship. It will be an easy day."

"Are you sure?"

"Positive. Miss Danielle needs help. If Mr. Patterson is waiting at the top, she should not go alone in case something happens."

There was some discussion about logistics, with Millie and Annette throwing out ideas. One thing was certain—Danielle would need backup, someone who was there to ensure she arrived at the meeting spot with the suitcase.

"Check with Cat," Annette said. "I think she has a little free time in St. Kitts. I'm guessing she might be interested in going with us."

"Will do." Millie's app chimed again. "I gotta get downstairs." She shoved the rest of the sandwich in her mouth and tossed the empty meal bag in the trash. "Thanks for the food. I'll be dreaming about those brownies tonight, Amit."

Millie reached the theater and found passengers already arriving for the upcoming show. She skirted the crowd and took the side stairs backstage. The ship's singers and dancers were crammed inside the dressing room, preparing for the evening's headliner show. The comedian stood off to the side, chatting with the magician.

She gave a quick wave and picked up the pace, making a beeline for her office. As Millie drew closer, she could hear loud voices. Andy's booming voice and another high-pitched voice, this one laced with sarcasm. "...tugboat of the seas." Another voice, this one deeper, repeated the sentence.

"I hope your entire show isn't about insulting Siren of the Seas," Andy replied. "I want to speak to Mervin and *only* Mervin."

"We talk as a team."

"And repeat the same thing?"

Millie peeked around the corner and found a tall thin man wearing a pale gray pinstriped suit casually leaning against the wall. Next to him, perched on top of a wooden barstool, was the dummy, dressed in an identical suit, with the same brown hair and smirking smile etched on his face. In other words, Flash was a miniature version of Mervin.

"Hello," she offered a tentative greeting as she stepped inside. "I hope I haven't kept you waiting."

Flash's head swiveled around. He blinked several times and let out a wolf whistle. "Who is this hot mama?"

Mervin repeated him. "Hot mama."

"This is the ship's cruise director, Millie Armati."

"Armati...Armati." Flash rolled his eyes. "Any connection to the captain?"

"I'm his wife." Millie wasn't sure who to extend a hand to, considering the dummy was doing most of the talking. She offered it to Mervin and wasn't surprised when Mervin lifted Flash's hand and shook. "Nice to meet you, Millie."

"Andy tells me you've been touring with Majestic Cruise Lines for several months now. Is there anything we can do to make your job easier?" she asked.

"Get me a raise. This gig pays peanuts," Flash whined.

"Peanuts," Mervin echoed.

"I'm sorry. I have no control over what you're being paid," Millie said. "Perhaps you should re-negotiate when your contract ends."

A breathless Felix appeared in the doorway. "It's showtime."

Millie consulted her watch. "Thanks, Felix. We'll chat after the show."

She tugged on the bottom of her jacket, cleared her throat and squared her shoulders. She'd done this dozens of times. Maybe even hundreds, but only a handful as the ship's official cruise director.

And opening night was important. It set the stage for the week. It was the passengers' first glimpse into what was in store for them. In other words, if the *Welcome Aboard* show bombed, passengers might be inclined to look for things to complain about and complaints were the last thing a newly minted cruise director needed.

Her welcome speech went off without a hitch, and she turned the stage over to the singers and dancers. Millie slipped behind the curtain, her heart swelling with pride as they danced and twirled, spun and sang, putting everything they had into the performance.

The crowd clapped along to a popular eighties tune, and she started to relax. It was going to be all right.

The comedian was up next. He took a few small jabs at the food, which was par for the course, praised the room stewards, and then suggested the bartenders add a little more booze to the mixed drinks.

Millie grabbed the microphone and thanked him for his performance. The magician was next. When it was time for Flash and Mervin to do their little ditty, she could feel her armpits grow damp.

They took the stage and Flash started it off by complaining about how he and Mervin always dressed the same. The dummy heckled several passengers until someone in the front row appeared to get his attention.

In fact, he zeroed in on the woman to the point Millie could feel a heat creep into her cheeks. She sensed someone stepping in next to her. It was Andy. "Well?"

"I'm on the fence about this guy," Millie muttered. "Where did you find him?"

"He came highly recommended by the head of entertainment."

"Meaning Mervin is probably a buddy of his."

"It could be. Hopefully, this is just a bumpy start," Andy said.

"He needs to lay off the lady in the first row."

But Flash didn't. In fact, he kept at her until the "Flash and Mervin show" left Millie no choice. She clenched her jaw and pulled the curtain aside. "It's time to reel them in."

Chapter 8

"Thank you for your very entertaining dialogue." Millie began propelling the ventriloquist and his rude dummy off the stage.

"Hang on." Flash and Mervin deftly sidestepped her. "I have one more joke."

"I can hardly wait to hear it." Millie forced a smile.

"It's time for Siren of the Seas to hire a ventriloquist for cruise director," Flash said. "All we have right now is a dummy."

The tasteless joke got a few chuckles. Millie, fed up with Flash and Mervin's antics, placed an ironclad grip on the man's arm and steered him toward the back. "Please be sure to keep an eye on the Cruise Ship Chronicles to find the location and time of Flash and Mervin's next show."

Felix sprang into action and helped whisk the troublesome duo away. She returned to center stage to end the show. "We hope you enjoy the rest of this evening's entertainment. The ship's crew and staff are working hard to bring you nonstop fun and activities as we travel to St. Kitts."

She rattled off a few more highlights of the evening's entertainment and the curtains closed. Millie did an about-face and caught Felix's eye as he stood nearby. "Where are they?"

"In your office. I figured you would want to chat with Mervin about his performance."

"Chat with him and drive home the point that his job isn't to insult our passengers."

Felix lowered his voice. "What's up with the dummy doing most of the talking and the guy being the echo in the room?"

"Your guess is as good as mine. Flash obviously runs the show."

"Good luck."

"Thanks. I'm going to need it." Millie strode toward her office door, slowing when she heard voices.

"You told me I needed to kick the funnies up a notch." Flash rolled his eyes. "How was I supposed to know it would get us into trouble?"

"Nothing but trouble." Mervin wagged his finger at the dummy while shaking his head. He cupped his hand to the dummy's ear and whispered something.

Millie stepped inside and cleared her throat. "Hello."

Flash's head spun around. "You were in a rush to get me and Merv off the stage."

"Because you were insulting passengers," Millie said bluntly. "I want to see the material for the rest of your shows."

"I'm not required to provide that to the cruise director," Flash haughtily replied.

"You're going to this time." Millie took the seat directly across from them. "Your show was in poor taste. If you were trying to be funny, you weren't. You were rude, condescending and, quite frankly, an embarrassment."

She tapped her scheduler app and scrolled through the screen. "You have a show tomorrow evening in the Paradise Lounge. I want a copy of the entire routine on my desk by nine o'clock tomorrow morning."

Mervin shoved his chair back. "Fine."

"Fine. We'll have it to you," Flash said.

"In fact, you might as well give me the rest. I want copies of all your materials for this cruise."

"Providing a copy isn't in the contract," Flash argued.

"Neither is being a jerk to our passengers," Millie snapped. "Either give me the material or I'm pulling you from the schedule and contacting

94

corporate to have you sent home at our first port stop."

Flash whispered something to Mervin, and then nodded. "We'll have a copy of everything on your desk by tomorrow morning."

"Thank you." Millie stood. "And if it was anything like the teaser you put on tonight, I suggest some heavy editing."

Flash looked away and Millie could've sworn the dummy rolled his eyes again. Without uttering another word, Flash and Mervin strolled out of her office, passing by Andy, who was on his way in.

"I heard loud voices. I take it you chatted with Mervin?"

"Mervin, but mostly with Flash. Do you have any suggestions about how I can get Mervin to talk and get the dummy to stop insulting people?"

"Perhaps you should ask him to provide you with a copy of his dialogue."

"Already done. I told him I wanted it on my desk by nine tomorrow morning, and I also told him to clean it up. We can't have them insulting passengers."

"He was coming on a little strong," Andy agreed. "How is Danielle? I heard she's down in medical."

"Someone attacked her in the cargo storage building right before we left port."

Andy's eyes widened. "Attacked her?"

"Thankfully, Sharky was nearby. He heard something, ran inside and found Danielle out cold on the floor."

"What was she doing in the cargo building?"

"Picking up a suitcase. She's going to be all right, but there's an issue with what was inside."

"Contraband stuff?"

"You could say that." Millie glanced over Andy's shoulder and lowered her voice. "Between you and me, Patterson found drugs hidden inside the suitcase."

Andy made a choking sound. "Danielle doesn't do drugs."

"Nope. It appears someone from her past was trying to trick her into transporting drugs to St. Kitts. Patterson is on it." Millie explained how the suitcase slipped through the cracks and made it on board the ship before the drug-sniffing dogs searched the storage building.

"How did Patterson know to look for drugs if the dogs didn't alert security?"

"Fin. Danielle asked me to bring the suitcase to her. I was in Sharky's office while he tracked it down. As soon as Fin got a whiff, he was all over it."

"Is Patterson going to lock her up pending an investigation?"

"I hope not. I think the plan is to set up a sting in St. Kitts. Danielle meets with the person who sent the suitcase. Patterson, his team, and more than likely the local authorities, will swoop in and apprehend him."

"It sounds risky. And where do you fit into all of this?"

Millie's eyes widened innocently. "What makes you think I'll be involved?"

Andy crossed his arms. "C'mon, Millie. If there's a mystery to be solved, you'll be involved."

"Danielle has helped me out a lot. I feel somewhat responsible to make sure she gets a fair shake. Besides, I might have a lead on a spot where the transaction could potentially take place. It's called Brimstone Hill National Fortress."

"Brimstone Hill," Andy repeated. "It's a somewhat remote World UNESCO site."

Millie perked up at the word "remote." "Remote? I kind of got that impression and now you've confirmed it. You've been there before?"

"If it's the place I'm thinking of, there are hairpin turns, switchback roads going back and forth all the way to the top of the hill." He pulled his cell phone from his pocket and tapped the screen. "This is it. There's only one way up to the fortress and one way back down."

"It sounds perfect." Millie darted around her desk and peered over his shoulder. "It looks like a pretty cool place."

"The views from the top are magnificent. It's well worth a visit."

"You sealed the deal." Millie made a mental note to run it by Patterson and thanked Andy for the information.

"I'm heading to my office. Donovan wants me to come up with a plan to reduce the cost of passengers' beverage packages."

"Translation…you're looking for ways to cut some corners."

"Trim costs, but not in a way the passengers will notice." Andy began rattling off statistics. "On a weekly voyage, we go through thousands of bottles of water."

Millie let out a low whistle. "Wow."

"On top of that we have juices, sodas, not to mention beer and other beverages. Donovan and I will be focusing on ways to reduce costs *and* eliminate waste."

"Sounds like a fun project. Maybe if you get the costs down, your plan will be the blueprint for the other cruise ships, other cruise lines, to become more efficient." Millie tilted her head. "Is your title finally official?"

He gave her a thumbs up. "On paper and on payroll. I'm the ship's activities and expenditures liaison."

"Sounds fancy," Millie teased. She quickly sobered. "The best part is you're doing better."

"It's like night and day. The stress of not running here and there almost twenty-four seven is helping bring my blood pressure down."

"I'm glad to hear it." Millie caught a movement out of the corner of her eye. It was Flash. "You can come in. The door is open."

The dummy and Mervin appeared. "Sorry to bother you."

"I was just leaving." Andy offered Millie an encouraging smile. He nodded to Flash and Mervin before making his way out of the office.

"Did you forget something?"

"I have tomorrow's material. I was going to slide it under the door, but noticed you were still here." While Flash did the talking, Mervin handed her a thick stack of papers.

"Thank you. I'll take a look at it to make sure it meets my, 'let's not insult and alienate the passengers' standards," Millie said.

"You're welcome." Flash's head spun around. "Merv and I were thinking about heading down to the crew lounge after the last show to grab a drink. Would you care to join us?"

"I'm on duty until late and then heading home."

"Maybe you could swing by after your shift ends," the dummy suggested.

"I'm married," Millie said bluntly. "Happily married to the ship's captain."

"If you change your mind..."

"I won't. I'll see you tomorrow." Millie watched as Mervin and Flash meandered out of her office.

She placed a light hand on the back of her neck. *Serenity now.* Something told her it was going to be a very long cruise with Flash and Mervin on board.

Chapter 9

Millie dashed upstairs for the Jingle Bell Ball and found Felix in full "Felix-mode," schmoozing the female passengers, flattering the husbands and entertaining them with a new dance move.

He caught Millie's eye and hurried over. "There you are. I was wondering what happened to you."

"Sorry. I got hung up in my office, among other places."

"I figured you were tossing Flash the dummy over the side of the ship," Felix joked.

"We had a nice chat. I can't have him insulting passengers," Millie said. "Hopefully, I've nipped his rude routine in the bud. I have his act for tomorrow and if I find anything even a smidgen condescending, I'm going to—what do the directors say?"

Felix made a slicing motion across his neck. "Put him on the chopping block."

"Both of them."

The chorus of voices grew louder and the line of past passengers waiting to enter the lounge snaked down the long hall.

"The natives are getting restless," Felix whispered.

"I'll be right back." Millie slipped inside where she found servers sporting festive elf hats standing near the entrance, food and beverage trays in hand, waiting for their special guests.

She stepped back out and gave Felix a thumbs up. "It's showtime. They're ready for us."

Millie opened the double set of doors and joined Felix in collecting invitations and thanking their guests for choosing Majestic Cruise Lines.

She knew many of them by name, and a few lingered, congratulating her on her promotion and asking about Andy.

The orchestra started to play *Jingle Bell Cruise,* an upbeat Christmas tune, and by the time Millie collected the final invitation, the party was in full swing. Glasses of champagne, mixed drinks, and sparkling water made their rounds.

The hors d'oeuvres were top-notch. Salmon and sushi, caprese salad skewers with a balsamic drizzle, gourmet pizza, and then the servers brought out the desserts. Several times, Millie recommended Amit's dark chocolate brownies.

Nic arrived and gave his speech, thanking the guests for their loyalty to the cruise line and handing out awards and special gifts to those who hit milestones.

Up next was introducing the officers, and Millie joined them onstage. She gazed around the room, beaming with pride, surrounded by what she considered the "best of the best."

With the introductions over, the orchestra started playing again and couples hit the dance floor.

"I haven't seen you all day."

Millie turned to find her husband standing behind her. "It's been...well, turnaround day. You know how it goes."

"How is Danielle?"

"She's going to be all right."

"I'm glad to hear it. Patterson filled me in earlier. It appears we have a concerning issue on our hands."

"Yes. Hopefully one that will be resolved soon."

"Have you been by the apartment to check out Scout's new and expanded balcony?"

"Not yet." *Siren of the Seas'* maintenance crew had been working on some small updates, repairs and renovations which could be completed while the ship was in port. One of those changes was expanding Nic and Millie's balcony, giving their small pup more "room to roam."

Millie's eyes lit. "How did it turn out? Does he like it?"

"He loves it." Nic grinned. "He's like a pup let loose in his favorite pet store."

A passenger arrived to chat. Nic stayed for a few minutes and then excused himself when Captain Vitale tracked him down and told him he was needed on the bridge.

Millie made her rounds, chatting with guests. The VIP party was one of her favorites. It was like catching up with old friends. Santa made an appearance, handing out candy canes and goody bags.

Finally, the festivities ended, and the party moved to the atrium, where the Christmas tree, filled with glittery ornaments and tons of tinsel, sat next to the makeshift stage. There was more live music and an even bigger crowd.

She hung back to help the staff straighten up and caught up with Joy. "Hey, Millie. How's it going?"

"Swimmingly," Millie joked.

"You have a lot of superfans on board the ship."

"Superfans. Friends. These VIP parties are like a family reunion." Millie reached for an empty glass. "How have you been?"

"Happy as a lark. I'll be taking a break soon, heading home to Divine, Kansas, to see my family."

"Good for you. And how is Donovan?"

Joy smiled sheepishly. "He's fine. We don't get to spend a lot of time together. Either he's working or I'm working. We can't seem to get our schedules to line up."

"But when you do, you have fun," Millie said.

"Yeah. I love life on board the ship."

"Isla mentioned you two plan to visit Brimstone Hill in St. Kitts. I'm almost certain I'll be tagging along as well."

"Sweet! Have you seen the place? I love UNESCO sites. In fact, I've made it my goal to visit every single one where we make a port stop." Joy rattled on about the fort, and her enthusiasm was contagious. Perhaps there was more than one reason for Millie to want to visit the special place.

After Joy walked away, Millie sent a quick text to Isla, asking her to sign Annette up for the excursion. She promptly replied and told her there were still plenty of spots if she could think of anyone else. Which left only one other person on Millie's list.

*****

Ocean Treasures, the ship's main gift shop, was deader than a doornail. Millie found her friend, Cat, in the back, folding shirts.

"Hey, Millie. I would ask you how you're doing, but I've already talked to Andy. He said the ventriloquist is giving you fits."

"Giving me fits. Insulting the passengers. Insulting me." Millie pursed her lips. "And the guy hardly ever talks. When he does, he echoes what the dummy says."

"That's kinda weird."

"Kinda weird *and* kinda creepy. We had a chat. Hopefully, he got the message and revised his entertainment material." Millie changed the subject. "How are you?"

Cat tipped her hand back and forth. "I'm glad we still have a few weeks left before the wedding. I'm getting the jitters and not in a good way."

Millie propped her elbow on the counter. "Because of Jay?"

"Because of Jay. Living in close quarters. Having to report to someone."

"Hold up." Millie cut her off. "You're making marriage sound like a jail sentence."

Cat groaned. "And I don't want it to. I love Andy. He's funny and thoughtful and sweet. I just…"

"Don't self-sabotage. You deserve to be happy. Keep reminding yourself of that. You're a wonderful person, Cat. Loving, loyal, caring, considerate. Is it because you're afraid that once you marry, Andy will change like Jay did?"

Her friend gave a small nod.

Millie drummed her fingers on the counter. "I understand where you're coming from, but Jay and Andy are two completely different people. Besides, as opposed to Jay, who isolated you and controlled you, there is no way Andy could try even if he wanted to. There are too many people. You have too many friends on board this ship."

"You're right, and I keep reminding myself of that." Cat pinched her index finger and thumb together. "But the teensy, tiny little spark in my brain keeps reminding me people change."

Millie grasped Cat's arm. "You'll never go through what you went through with Jay. It's time for you to let yourself be happy, to love someone and live your best life."

"I will. I'm trying. Thanks for the pep talk."

"You're welcome. Speaking of living your best life, Joy, Annette, Isla, Danielle and I are taking the Brimstone Hill Fortress morning excursion when we reach St. Kitts. Why don't you come with us? We'll make it a girl's day out."

"Brimstone Hill?" Cat wrinkled her nose. "Isn't that the twisty, turning trip to the tippy top of an old fort?"

"Yep. Sounds like fun, huh?"

"I..."

"C'mon," Millie persuaded. "We hardly ever all get to hang out. This might be your last hurrah as a single woman. The gift shop is closed while we're in port, so there's no excuse."

"Okay. Fine," Cat relented. "I'll go with you."

"Great." Before her friend could change her mind, Millie whipped her cell phone out and sent another text to Isla, adding Cat to the list. "This will be so much fun, all except for the part where Danielle meets up with a drug dealer."

Chapter 10

The rest of Millie's evening flew by. She traveled forward to aft, top to bottom, checking on events, hosting the second *Welcome Aboard* show where, thankfully, Mervin and Flash had toned down their act.

Flash got one small dig in on a passenger in a second row aisle seat, but kept the rest of the show light and entertaining and even avoided targeting Millie when she joined him to wrap it up.

She hosted a late-night karaoke, checked in at the nightclub, and then finally headed home.

Millie stepped onto the bridge and lingered momentarily, savoring the peacefulness...the soft lighting, the steady, familiar hum of the equipment.

It was like night and day—the hustle and bustle of the ship's activities as opposed to the bridge where it was calm, orderly and almost always quiet.

She clasped her hands. *Thank you, God, for another good day. Thank you for keeping Danielle from being seriously injured. Please help us clear her name.*

She opened her eyes and found Nic and Craig McMasters standing near the control panel, talking in low voices. Millie wandered over, waiting for them to finish.

"Hello, Millie." The ship's Scottish first officer greeted her. "You look puggled this evening."

"Puggled as in a pup?"

Nic chuckled. "It's Scottish for tired."

"Oh. Tired. I'm definitely puggled," Millie repeated. "In fact, I'll probably be puggled tomorrow and the day after and the day after that."

"I noticed earlier you have some time off during our port stop in St. Kitts. Have you made plans?" Nic asked.

"Tentatively. I thought you were scheduled to work full shifts."

"I am, although I've managed to sneak in a few hours off on Wednesday and have something special planned for us," her husband said. "Which means you're free to hang out at home or do whatever in St. Kitts."

"Isla invited me to join her and some others for an early morning excursion."

Nic rubbed the stubble on his chin. "Does it have anything to do with Danielle?"

"Maybe a smidgen." Millie pinched her thumb and index finger together.

"I don't think you should become involved. Patterson will handle it."

"I'm sure he will. I might be jumping the gun, but I think Brimstone Hill is the optimal meeting spot. Danielle shouldn't go there alone. Annette, Cat, and I will tag along for moral support."

"Patterson hasn't confirmed the meeting location," Nic said.

"Not yet, but it makes the most sense, at least from a security standpoint."

Nic started to say something, and Millie hurried on. "Besides, Danielle works under me now. She's an important member of the entertainment team. It's in my best interest to make sure the issue is resolved."

"True." Nic sighed heavily, fully aware he was losing the argument. "You're done for the day?"

"Done for the day and excited to check out Scout's expanded space." Millie touched Nic's hand. "When will you be heading home?"

"Within the next few minutes, as soon as my replacement arrives."

"See you then. Have a nice night, Craig."

"You too Millie."

She trekked down the hall and eased the apartment door open. Scout, their teacup yorkie, stood on the other side. He pounced on her shoe and pranced around, all the while yapping excitedly.

She bent down, intending to scoop him up, but Scout was too fast. He took off, running straight toward the sliding glass doors.

"You can't wait to show me around." Millie trailed after her pup, and as soon as she opened the door, he scampered out of sight.

"I'm going to lose you out here." Millie flipped the lights on, illuminating the improved balcony. A patch of dirt replaced Scout's artificial turf with real grass covering the top. There was even a small bed of blooming flowers.

Opposite the grassy area, where their original deck ended, was a pair of new deck chairs with a table tucked in between.

To the left of the table and chairs was a small inflatable pool, waiting to be filled. A bin of brightly colored plastic balls sat next to the pool. A new partition of plexiglass had been added to the bottom of the railing to keep Scout safe and prevent his toys from falling over the side.

Millie caught up with her pup, who was standing in the empty pool. "You want to go swimming?" she laughed. "It's a little late, but maybe tomorrow."

Nic appeared in the doorway. "Well? What do you think?"

"I think it's wonderful," Millie said. "We have room for us, room for Scout, a spot for him to stretch his legs. We should've done this sooner."

"I agree." Nic placed a light kiss on his wife's forehead. "We never finished our conversation about Danielle's situation. Patterson mentioned she's waiting to contact the suitcase's owner."

"Yep. We're at a standstill until she finalizes her plan to meet Emilio, her brother's drug-dealing friend."

"And when is this supposed to take place?"

"As soon as we arrive in St. Kitts," Millie said. "I think Patterson should seriously consider Brimstone Hill National Fortress. It's in a more remote and isolated area of the island, meaning he'll have fewer potential casualties."

"As far as, if the exchange goes south, there won't be as many innocent bystanders possibly getting in harm's way." Nic's jaw tightened.

"You don't like the idea of me being involved."

"Of course, not. But I also know I can't stop you."

Millie wisely changed the subject. "Are you hungry? Would you like me to fix you a sandwich? Maybe a wrap?"

"Whatever sounds good to you." Nic followed her into the kitchen. "Something quick and easy and not too heavy."

While Millie fixed sandwiches, she and Nic discussed the ship's revised itinerary.

After finishing, they returned to their private outdoor oasis. The couple prayed over their food and chatted about Cat and Andy's upcoming wedding, which Nic would be officiating on New Year's Eve.

Millie didn't mention Cat's cold feet. She was confident that by the time the wedding rolled around, her friend would overcome her anxiety.

The couple lingered after they finished eating. It was one of Millie's favorite times of the day. The quiet hours, quiet moments she spent with Nic, catching up.

She hoped Cat and Andy could look forward to the same loving relationship, someone who always had their back, someone to share life's ups and downs. In other words, she hoped their later years would be the best years.

Finally, Nic reluctantly stood. "It's getting late. We should probably head to bed."

Millie stifled a yawn. "Sea days equals extra entertainment. It will be all hands on deck tomorrow and the next day." She reached for the empty dishes, and Nic stopped her. "You made dinner. I'll clean up while you get ready for bed."

By the time she finished washing up, brushing her teeth and swapping out her work clothes for pajamas, Nic and Scout were waiting in the bedroom.

They traded places. Nic emerged from the bathroom and found their pup had already claimed his favorite spot—smack dab between their heads at the top of the bed.

The couple prayed for a smooth voyage and then prayed for Danielle to make a full recovery. After finishing, Millie added an extra prayer they would be able to track down the cocaine's rightful owner. Last, but not least, she prayed Danielle would finally find peace and let go of the guilt she held onto over Casey's death.

Chapter 11

Millie was up and out the door early the next morning for a staff meeting, followed by *Fun Times at Nine with Millie*, a new live on-air show which replaced *Adventures at Eight with Andy*.

Her "guest of the day" was the ship's comedian who kept it clean with jokes for folks and kids alike.

After a quick trip to the crew cafeteria for breakfast, Millie began a round of trivia, something she was reluctant to relinquish despite her added responsibilities.

The morning flew by, filled with mini golf, poolside activities, and even a scavenger hunt. She popped into the children's area, filled with eight to twelve-year-olds who were working on a Christmas skit for their parents.

Near noon, Millie headed down to the medical center to check on Danielle. She found her friend in her room, dressed and pacing the floor.

"Hey, there," Millie greeted her as she stepped inside. "It looks like you're raring to go."

"Doctor Gundervan is a stickler for following the rules. He's keeping me hostage until he gives me one final examination and signs off on my stay."

"Hostage?" Millie laughed. "It's for your own good."

"I know, but it's boring in here. There's nothing to do. I've watched your nine o'clock morning show half a dozen times already."

"I have to agree the ship's television entertainment is limited."

"More like non-existent. The internet is slower than molasses." Danielle grimaced. "I'm whining, aren't I?"

"A little."

"Sorry. It's tough sitting here, that's all."

Doctor Gundervan appeared. "The nurse said you're itching for me to release you."

"Itching, scratching, ready to pop out the porthole and sneak out," Danielle joked.

"I'll wait for you up front." Millie made her way to the waiting room. The minutes ticked by and she was beginning to think the doctor wasn't going to give Danielle a clean bill of health.

Finally, she appeared, with Doctor Gundervan close behind. The grumpy look was long gone. "I'm ready to blow this popsicle stand."

Millie thanked the doctor. She linked arms with Danielle and they meandered down the hall. "See? That wasn't so bad."

"I suppose not, and I should be grateful." Danielle slowed when they reached the crew dining room. "Do you mind if we grab a bite to eat? The food back there leaves a lot to be desired."

"Let's do one better." Millie consulted her watch. "The lunch rush is wrapping up. I'm sure Annette has a delicious dish or two to tempt you."

"I like your way of thinking."

The women changed direction and began making their way to the bank of elevators. Millie pushed the button and waited for the doors to open.

"You're taking the elevator?" Danielle asked.

"I would rather take the stairs, but I think you need to take it easy today."

They stepped inside and were joined by a trio of crewmembers who got off on deck four. It was their turn when they reached deck seven, the main galley deck, and made the short trek down the long corridor to the galley's crewmember entrance.

The place was a beehive of activity with kitchen staff bustling back and forth.

"This might not have been the best idea," Millie whispered.

"Let's go."

The women began backing out when Annette bustled around the corner. She did a double take and hustled over. "Danielle. I heard about your conk on the head. How are you feeling?"

"Much better now that I'm out of the medical center. I'll feel even better when I don't have a suitcase of cocaine hanging over my head."

"Speaking of which, I've been giving it some thought," Millie said.

"Uh-oh. Here we go," Annette teased.

"Seriously. I think I have the perfect plan."

Danielle pointedly patted her stomach. "Food first. Plan of action second."

"Right." Millie clasped her hands. "We were going to grab a bite to eat. I didn't realize this place would be such a madhouse, although I should've known better."

Annette waved dismissively. "This is nothing. What can I get you?"

"What do you have?" Danielle eyed the staging area and stainless-steel shelves filled with food.

"Soups, salads, sandwiches. I highly recommend the chicken pasta fettuccine," Annette said.

"It sounds delicious." Danielle licked her lips. "Mind if I grab a plate?"

"Make it two," Millie said.

"How about three? I haven't taken my break yet. We'll find a quiet corner and talk about the sting." Annette grabbed a tray, loaded it with three plates of pasta and led her friends to a corner table with folding chairs.

"Millie kind of filled me in, but I want to hear your version of what went down regarding the suitcase," Annette said.

"Emilio, my brother's friend, contacted me out-of-the-blue. He said he was moving to St. Kitts and wanted to return some of my brother's things. I gave him the port address and wired him some cash to cover the shipping." Danielle told them Emilio texted her with the suitcase's arrival date, which is when she went to the cargo warehouse to pick it up.

"I've been in the cargo storage area during turnaround day. How on earth did you find the suitcase?" Annette asked.

"It wasn't easy. Thankfully, it had a shipping label with my name on it. Emilio also told me he tied a green and white bandana around the handle."

"There was no return address," Millie said.

Danielle twirled her fork and took a big bite of pasta. "Nope. There wasn't."

"Because Emilio didn't want to risk having the suitcase traced back to him," Annette theorized.

"That's what I'm thinking." Danielle continued. "So, I went to grab the bag. I heard a noise. The next thing I know, I'm flat on my back. I have a splitting headache and Sharky is hovering over me."

"But the suitcase was still there." Annette tore off a chunk of her breadstick.

"I think Sharky scared them off," Millie said. "My guess is someone knew about the suitcase, planned to intercept it before Danielle picked it up and wasn't able to because Sharky showed up."

"Hmmm." Annette cleared her throat.

"What are you thinking?" Millie asked.

"Who has access to the cargo storage area?"

"Crewmembers, the port authority and the police."

"And the drug-sniffing dogs hadn't yet made it."

"Because they only come in after everything is in the cargo area, ready to be checked." Danielle blinked rapidly. "Which means there was a narrow window of time for the cargo area to be filled and ready before the drug-sniffing dogs arrived."

"And who would have that information?"

"Ship employees," Danielle and Millie said in unison.

"Which means if someone is hot after the suitcase and its contents, that person works for the cruise lines," Annette said.

"Either as a shore-side employee or someone who works on board this ship." Millie could feel her scalp tingle. Whoever had attempted to intercept the suitcase and attacked Danielle could very well be on board the *Siren of the Seas*. "This adds a whole new level of concern."

"They won't be able to get their hands on the suitcase," Danielle said. "Patterson wouldn't let me touch my brother's things."

"Because it's potential evidence," Annette reminded her. "He can't."

"We need to figure out if anyone has been tampering with the luggage, the contraband holding room, or any other area of the ship where items brought on board are stored. I know one person who can give us the information we need," Millie said.

"Sharky." Danielle polished off the rest of her food.

"Bingo." Millie scraped the last bite of pasta from the bottom of her plate. "Thank you for the pasta. It was delicious."

"I'm glad you enjoyed it."

Millie, with Danielle by her side, made a beeline for the maintenance office. Sharky wasn't around and it took a few minutes for them to track him down.

The women finally located him inside the recycling center. The Flamethrower, Sharky's scooter, was parked nearby, with Fin lounging in the front basket.

Millie patted the cat's head and waited until he finished talking to a worker.

"Hey, Danielle, Millie." He gave a quick wave and hurried over. "How's the old noggin?" Sharky tapped the side of his head.

"Feeling much better," Danielle said. "Thank you for rescuing me. Who knows what would've happened if you hadn't shown up."

"You're welcome," Sharky said. "And the suitcase?"

"Patterson has it safely stored somewhere," Millie said. "Which is why we're here. We were just talking to Annette, trying to put the pieces together and have a couple of questions."

"And maybe I have a couple of answers," Sharky quipped.

"Who has access to the cargo storage area?" Danielle asked.

"The ship's crewmembers."

"What about the contracted stevedores?"

"They have access, as well as the security guards and port personnel."

"But not the public," Millie said.

"Nope. It's a restricted area, accessible only by those I mentioned."

"So, whoever attacked Danielle was a ship employee, a port employee, or someone who works in security."

"Correct."

"Assuming they knew what was hidden inside the suitcase, they would have only a small timeframe to grab the goods and get out before the drug-sniffing dogs arrived."

"Yeah. Someone either got very lucky or they knew exactly when the goods would be in place and ready to load onto the ship."

"That's what we were thinking," Millie said. "Has anyone been messing around the storage areas?"

Sharky's jaw dropped. "Yeah. Someone tore through the lost and found. In fact, I had a staff meeting this morning, reminding my guys about making sure they didn't make a mess. No one admitted responsibility."

"As in tore through lost and found looking for something?"

"I've never seen them trash the place before, which is why I called a meeting. I figured it was one of the new guys. We have a few."

Millie blew air through thinned lips. "I don't think it was one of your new guys. I think it was someone who was searching for a black suitcase with a green and white cloth tied around the handle."

"What about cameras?" Danielle asked. "Do you have cameras near the lost and found area?"

"Sure do." Sharky led them out of the recycling center, through a maze of corridors to an area Millie had never been in before. It was next to the contraband room but more accessible, with a stairwell only steps away.

Millie gauged the distance between the two. Someone could have easily sneaked down the stairs, rummaged around inside the lost and found and sneaked back out without ever being seen.

Sharky pointed to a camera overhead. "See there?"

Danielle stepped directly beneath it. "It's aimed toward the corridor."

"And not the side stairwell," Millie added.

"I'll check the footage. It happened last night, after the ship left port."

Millie's app chimed. "I gotta get going. Let me know if you find anything." She waited until she and Danielle exited the storage area. "Well?"

"I think someone on board this ship is after that suitcase."

"Me too. I hate to sleuth and run, but I'm hosting the champagne art auction."

"And I'm on schedule for a mix and mingles singles party."

"Which is down the corridor from my next event. We'll run up there together," Millie said.

"Doctor Gundervan gave me some pain reliever in case my headache comes back. I want to drop the pills off at home first."

The women took the stairs up one deck to the crew's quarters and trekked down the hall to Danielle's cabin.

She started to slip her keycard in the slot and abruptly stopped. "What in the world?"

Chapter 12

A sinking feeling settled in the pit of Millie's stomach when she saw Danielle's damaged cabin door. "Your roommate, Carlah, busted down your door?"

"Carlah is on break and won't be back until January." Danielle braced herself and took a tentative step inside.

Millie eased in next to her friend, her heart plummeting at the cramped quarters now in shambles. "It looks like the person who is after the suitcase knows you have it."

"You mean *had* it, for like a minute before we parted ways after my attack." Danielle scooped up a pile of socks. "Whoever is doing this is really starting to tick me off. Emilio has some serious explaining to do. Why tear my cabin apart? Obviously, they can see the suitcase isn't here."

"Maybe whoever it is thinks you already emptied the contents. Hang on." Millie pulled her cell phone from her pocket and snapped pictures of the cabin. "When we're done, I'm going to forward these to Patterson to let him know what's going on." She grabbed a handful of shirts and began folding them.

The women made quick work of straightening the cabin and, as Millie had pointed out, nothing was destroyed, just disturbed—in a major way.

"We need to let Patterson know so he can check the corridor cameras." Millie sent a quick text and attached a picture. "He's on his way. I'll wait for him in the hall."

Danielle trailed after her. "The cameras had to have caught something."

"That's what I'm thinking." The women walked to the end of the hall and then backtracked.

Footsteps echoed and Patterson, along with Oscar, the director of security, appeared. "How's it looking?"

"Like I'll need a new door." Danielle pointed to the bent doorframe and loose lock. "It won't even shut all the way."

"I'll call maintenance and have them get down here right away." Oscar reached for his radio while the head of security followed the women inside.

Patterson did a quick tour while Millie filled him in on what Sharky had told them, how someone had rummaged through the lost and found. "At first, he thought it was one of the new guys making the mess. Did you find anything on the cargo area cameras?"

"We spotted a person we believe may have been Danielle's attacker. Unfortunately, we weren't able to get a clear look. Whoever it was, knew where the cameras were located."

"Again, an inside job," Millie said.

Danielle's scheduling app chimed. "I'm going to be late for my singles party."

"You go on. I'll have Oscar guard your cabin until maintenance arrives to repair the door," Patterson promised.

"Thank you. Hopefully, you'll be able to see something on the cameras, either here or in the lost and found area."

"I'm on it."

Millie and Danielle headed out, parting ways near the bank of elevators with Millie making her way to the champagne art auction.

The event kicked off with a rapid-fire closeout sale and Millie's mind wandered. Someone on board the ship knew about the suitcase and its contents, and something told her Emilio held the key.

The event ended, and Millie ran upstairs to the specialty restaurant's kitchen, to help host *Culinary Creations by Annette.*

The head of food and beverage was trying something new—a hands-on culinary class which offered passengers and participants the opportunity to help create delicious dishes.

Millie plucked an apron off the hook and caught up with her friend near the prep station. "What's on the menu today?"

"Crispy chicken cordon bleu finished off by toasting them in my fancy new set of portable salamander ovens," Annette said.

"It sounds yummy." Millie ran back to The Vine's entrance and greeted the guests, directing them to the kitchen. The last attendee arrived, and she returned to help.

Annette was quickly becoming an old pro at her new show and had even printed recipe cards for the guests to take home. Millie made sure the beverages were flowing and snapped action shots of the "chefs" as they prepared their special dishes.

"While I finish rolling the last batch of chicken in breadcrumbs, I'm going to ask our cruise director,

Millie, to crisp the entrées in the salamander ovens," Annette explained.

Millie grabbed one of the recipe cards, noting the crisping instructions, and turned both ovens on. She transferred the first batch of cordon bleu to the toasting trays and then eased them onto the racks.

"We're out of cabernet." A woman waved her empty wineglass in the air.

"I'll go grab some from the wine cellar." Millie hurried off to pick up a few more bottles and hustled back into the kitchen. She found a wine opener and began uncorking a bottle when a burnt smell caught her attention.

"Crud." Millie dropped the opener on the counter and raced across the room, horrified to discover wisps of smoke were pouring out of one of the salamanders. She unplugged the oven, and instinctively flung the door open. A big puff of smoke billowed out.

"The smoke alarm." Annette jogged around the counter, frantically waving her arms.

Beep. Beep. Beep. The kitchen's smoke alarm blared loudly.

"Shut the door!" Annette yelled.

Unfortunately, Millie couldn't hear over the blaring alarm.

Her friend shoved her aside, lunged forward and slammed the salamander door shut. In one swift move, she grabbed a pair of oven mitts, carried the still smoking appliance away from the alarm and set it on the floor.

Meanwhile, Amit grabbed a baking sheet and began fanning the alarm to clear the air.

Before Millie could react, a small army of safety crewmembers brandishing fire extinguishers raced into the kitchen.

The crew nearly collided with a group of wide-eyed guests who huddled off to the side, attempting to stay out of the way.

What could only be described as pure chaos ensued as the safety team split up, trying to figure out where the smoke was coming from.

Annette hopped on a chair, stuck her fingers in her mouth, and whistled loudly.

It got quiet. All except for the smoke alarm which Millie could've sworn grew louder by the second.

"We had a small fire in the salamander!" Annette yelled. "Someone, please shut the alarm off."

A safety team member carried a ladder from the storage area, scrambled to the top, and pressed the alarm's button.

While he reset the alarm, another team member grabbed his radio and announced an all-clear to the rest of the ship's crew.

"What happened?" the crewmember asked after giving the all-clear signal.

"I accidentally left the ovens unattended," Millie said in a small voice. "I'm sorry."

Annette picked up the salamander and set it on the counter. "Our first batch of cordon bleu is toast. Thank goodness we have an extra batch."

With the potential crisis averted, Millie apologized profusely as she followed the ship's safety team out of The Vine's kitchen.

Amit tracked down another oven and suggested he supervise the toasting, to which Millie wholeheartedly agreed.

The culinary class wrapped up, and the attendees headed into the dining room to enjoy the fruits of their labor, where several servers were on hand to offer side dishes and more drinks, leaving Millie, Amit, and Annette alone in the kitchen.

"I'm sorry I ruined your class," Millie said. "I got distracted and left the ovens unattended."

"The good news is it gave the safety team a legit exercise in responding to a fire threat. The guests will never forget how the cruise director almost burned the kitchen down and I'm pretty sure you're going to take a little ribbing about it," Annette said.

"I'm sure I will."

Thankfully, the rest of the class wrapped up without further incident, and Millie began her early evening schedule of events.

Danielle caught up with her during break time. "Patterson sent me a copy of the surveillance video from outside my cabin. It's on my cell phone."

"That was fast. Mind if I take a look?"

"Not at all." Danielle tapped the screen and handed her the phone.

Millie pressed the play button and watched as a medium-build man wearing a dark jacket and black knit cap appeared. "It's hard to see."

"It is. I was thinking about forwarding it to my email and watching it on my computer."

"I'm on break. Let's head up to my place. I'll fix us something to eat. We can check on Scout and watch the video on my laptop."

"As long as you don't set your apartment on fire," Danielle teased.

"Great," Millie groaned. "You heard."

"Me, along with probably every other crewmember on board the ship. I mean, when you hear bravo, bravo, bravo and The Vines restaurant being announced, it wasn't hard to figure out something went wrong during Annette's culinary class."

"It came across *everyone's* radio?" Millie could feel the tips of her ears burn.

"Considering I'm not part of the safety team and I heard it, my guess would be yes. So what happened?"

"I was making sure the cordon bleu entrees were nicely toasted in the salamanders. I got distracted by a guest who was asking for more wine, headed to the wine cellar and forgot all about the toasting breadcrumbs. By the time I got back, it was smoking." Millie told her she made the mistake of opening the oven door. "A big black cloud of smoke poured out. As luck would have it, the galley's detector happened to be directly above it."

"Tell you what, I'll swap out my craft class for the next culinary creations," Danielle joked.

"I might take you up on that." Millie patted her pocket. "Are you ready to head to my place? I promise I won't burn our food."

"It's a deal."

The women strolled to the other end of the ship, down to the bridge deck, and stepped inside where they found Nic, along with several other ship's officers, seated at the conference table.

Millie gave a quick wave, eager to avoid being questioned about the oven incident. But it wasn't to be.

"Hey, Millie." Nic waved her over.

Millie changed direction and reluctantly crossed the bridge. "Hello."

"We heard you had an exciting day."

"If you call setting off the fire alarm exciting, then I guess you could say so."

Danielle joined her. "The good news is the safety crew was on it."

"Boy, were they ever," Millie said.

Nic's eyes twinkled with mischief. "Remind me to check the apartment's smoke alarms later."

Millie playfully nudged him. "Very funny. It could have happened to anyone."

Nic sobered. "I'm glad it was only a small oven and the ship, the crew and our passengers are safe."

"Me too. On a positive note, it was an excellent exercise in emergency drills." A slow smile spread across her face as a thought occurred to Millie. "Does that mean you're going to do all the cooking now?"

"No way." Nic wagged a finger. "You're not getting off that easy."

"I'll let you get back to your meeting." Millie, with Danielle by her side, headed into the apartment.

Scout met them in the hall. He promptly trotted to the slider and gave them his saddest puppy dog eyes.

"I'm sure you're itching to go out. Let's give Danielle a tour." Millie unlocked the door and they followed the pup onto the balcony. "Well? What do you think?"

"This is awesome." Danielle spun in a slow circle. "Fresh air. Sunshine. I wish I had a balcony."

"I'll be happy to share mine with you." Millie glanced at her watch. "We don't have a lot of time. Do you mind if I order room service instead of scrounging around for food?"

"Not at all."

Millie stepped inside to place the order. Danielle trailed behind, waiting for her to finish.

"I think Scout would like to play in his pool. Is it okay if I put a little water in it?"

"Sure. He can splash around while we eat." Millie carried several pitchers of warm tap water to the pool.

Scout promptly hopped inside and began splashing around.

Their food arrived, and the friends dined alfresco, savoring the balmy ocean breezes. Off in the distance, Millie glimpsed another cruise ship. "We have one more sea day before we reach St. Kitts."

"I almost wish we were getting there tomorrow so I can get this over with," Danielle said. "I did some research on Brimstone Hill. It looks like the perfect spot to meet Emilio. I mentioned it to Patterson and after he checked it out, he agreed."

"Good. From what I found out I think so too. Thanks to Isla, we have it all lined up. You, me, Isla, Joy, Cat and Annette." Millie reached for a French fry and dipped it in catsup. "We need to figure out who conked you on the head and broke into your cabin. I wonder if Sharky caught anything on the cameras down by the lost and found."

"As soon as we finish eating, I'll call him," Danielle said.

Scout frolicked in his pool, dashing in and out while begging for small slivers of meat and treats.

With dinner out of the way, the women returned inside and settled in front of the computer.

"I'm gonna sit on this side so I can keep an eye on Scout in his pool." Millie placed a folding chair near the balcony door.

"I'll try to find Sharky." Danielle called down to the maintenance office and got him on her first attempt. "I have you on speaker. I'm here with Millie. Did you catch anything on the lost and found surveillance cameras?"

"Yeah. It's kinda fuzzy, but I have a shot of some guy wearing a dark jacket and knit hat digging through the stuff. It doesn't look like one of my guys. Of course, it's hard to tell since he was wearing a jacket and hat."

"Sounds like the same person who busted down my cabin door."

Sharky made a choking sound. "Someone broke into your cabin?"

"Broke in and tore it apart," Danielle said. "Would you mind sending me a copy of the video?"

Sharky grew quiet, and Millie could hear tapping on the other end. "You should have it."

Danielle's cell phone chirped. "Got it. Thanks, Sharky."

After hanging up, Danielle forwarded both videos, the one from Patterson and the one Sharky had sent, to Millie's email.

Millie clicked on the first video, the one outside Danielle's cabin, and enlarged the frame. There wasn't much to go on. It was a grainy image of what appeared to be a man. He was wearing a dark jacket, jeans and a knit hat.

The man checked both ends of the hall before approaching Danielle's door. Lifting one foot and leaning back, he kicked the door once and then a second time before it flew open.

The video ended and Millie clicked on the one Sharky had sent. She leaned in, studying the clip of a man digging through the stuff. "I'm almost positive this is the same person. I want to replay the one of the guy kicking your door in."

Danielle scooched closer while Millie replayed it. "It's hard to see what they look like."

The video ended, and Millie leaned back in her chair. "Same person, same clothing, looking for the same thing."

Danielle pressed her palms together. "Could you play Sharky's surveillance video one more time?"

"Sure." Millie hit the play button again.

"Stop."

Millie paused the video.

"There," Danielle said excitedly. "I think I found our first clue."

Chapter 13

Millie adjusted her reading glasses, studying the image of a person clad in black who was sifting through the lost and found items. "What am I missing?"

"There." Danielle pointed to a reflective logo on the person's jacket. "They have some sort of logo."

"You're right." She double-clicked on the image, which only made the logo blurrier. "I can't tell what it is. It looks a little familiar, like maybe I've seen it somewhere before."

"On a passenger?"

"Maybe. I suppose it's possible a passenger was digging around in lost and found, although they're supposed to have someone, a crewmember, accompany them." Millie wasn't convinced the person they caught on camera was a ship's passenger. "Let's look at the video of your cabin door being kicked in again."

She switched screens and began playing the corridor surveillance camera footage. "I can't tell if this person is wearing the same jacket, although it looks a lot like it."

They finished watching the video, and Millie slid the progress bar until she found what she thought was the optimal angle. She did a "print screen" shot and then forwarded it to her phone.

"What are you doing?" Danielle asked.

"Taking a screenshot of the jacket. There's something about it." Millie pulled up the lost and found recording, tracked down the frame containing the jacket's emblem and took another screenshot. "I'm almost positive I've seen this jacket somewhere, either on a passenger or maybe in the gift shop."

"That's it." Danielle snapped her fingers. "Maybe it's a jacket we sell in the gift shop, and Cat can give us a list of passengers who bought one."

"You might be onto something, Danielle." A flash of brown caught Millie's eye. It was Scout, soaking wet, sneaking past them and into the living room.

Millie sprang to her feet, snatched the towel off the deck chair, and wrapped it around her pup.

Scout wiggled and squirmed, but Millie kept a tight grip as she dried him off. "I take it you enjoyed your dip in the pool?"

Yip.

Danielle reluctantly stood. "It's time for me to get back to work."

Millie followed her to the door. "What time are you calling Emilio Tuesday morning?"

"Right after our staff meeting. Around eight."

"Which should work out perfectly. We're meeting at nine at the end of the dock for the

Brimstone Hill excursion," Millie said. "Do you mind if I listen in on the call?"

"Not at all. Patterson plans on being there. The more the merrier."

Danielle reached for the doorknob. "All I wanted was to get a small piece of my brother back. I should have known this would backfire, especially dealing with someone like Emilio."

Millie shifted Scout to her other arm and patted Danielle's shoulder. "I know how much you loved Casey and I'm sure he loved you. You'll get his things back. Patterson won't keep them forever."

"I hope not. I gotta get going."

After Danielle left, Millie said a small prayer for her, that she would stop blaming herself for her brother's death.

She fed Scout and then packed up his stroller. "How would you like to help with bingo and trivia?"

Scout finished his food in record time and promptly plopped down in front of the door.

"I guess you're ready to go. Let's get this entertainment show on the road."

*****

Millie, with Scout by her side, flew through her evening schedule, from bingo to trivia. They even hosted a holiday craft class. She caught up with Felix to co-host an evening round of their holiday scavenger hunt, *Christmas Cruise Clues*.

"Hey there, Scout." Felix patted his head. "Look at you...all puffy and fluffy."

"He was playing in his pool."

"He's one lucky little pup." Felix rubbed his hands together. "Are you ready for our holiday scavenger hunt?"

"More than ready. What do you have in mind?" Felix had volunteered to help coordinate the holiday season's scavenger hunt, and Millie was grateful for the helping hand.

"I thought you'd never ask. This is what I came up with." Felix handed her a clipboard, and Millie studied the list.

Eight tiny reindeer.

Red and green ornaments.

Santa and his sleigh.

A snowman.

Five golden rings.

A passenger with Santa's beard.

A picture of snow—artificial or real.

Gingerbread house.

Nativity scene.

Candy cane.

An elf hat.

Millie finished skimming the list with twenty-five items in all. "You have me stumped, at least on one item."

"Which one?"

"The nativity scene."

"Seriously?" Felix's jaw dropped. "When's the last time you stopped by Sky Chapel?"

"It's been a few days."

"You need to get up there. Pastor Pete put together a gorgeous nativity scene. I have no idea where he got the goods, but it's something special."

"I would love to see it. Thanks for the heads up." Millie consulted her watch. "I'm having second thoughts about awarding specialty coffee coupons. The coffee coupons have been played out."

"You must have read my mind." Felix took the clipboard from Millie and pulled a small stack of papers from the back. "I had some new coupons printed earlier today. What do you think about a trip to Celebrations to pick up one of those decadent brownies Amit created, or maybe even a festive Christmas cookie?"

"What a great idea." Millie squeezed his arm. "What would I do without you, Felix? You and Danielle."

"Be running around like a chicken with your head cut off." Felix tucked the coupons back under the clip. "I ran into Isla earlier. She mentioned something about you and a bunch of others visiting Brimstone Hill Tuesday morning."

"We are." Millie ticked off the list. "Annette, Joy, Isla, Danielle and maybe even Cat. You have time off in St. Kitts. What are your plans?"

Felix gave her a thumbs down. "A big, fat nothing. Do you mind if I tag along? I mean, I don't want to butt in…"

"Not at all. We're setting up a small sting involving Patterson and Danielle. I don't see why you can't come along."

"Oh." Felix clapped his hands. "A Millie adventure," he sing-songed. "It sounds like fun. Count me in."

"I'm not sure I would use the word fun, but it could very well be an adventure."

Scout began circling his stroller as several passengers arrived for the scavenger hunt. A few stopped by to say hello, and the pup basked in their adoration.

"Isn't he the most adorable miniature yorkie?" a woman gushed. "I didn't know dogs were allowed on board."

"They're not," Millie said. "The captain made an exception for Scout. He's our unofficial mascot."

The other attendees trickled in, and Millie and Scout stood off to the side, giving Felix ample room to run the show. Soon, the participants were on their way to hunt down the Christmas items.

While they were gone, Millie and Felix chatted about Brimstone Hill. "We're meeting at the end of the pier at nine."

"I'll be there with bells on." Felix reached for his phone and tapped the screen. "Isla is such a doll. She said Cat confirmed and that she also signed me up. Cat and I snagged the last two spots."

"Even better. It sounds like it will just be us."

The contest ended and Millie thanked Felix for his help before swinging by the apartment to drop Scout off. She wrapped up her late night hosting. By the time her shift finally ended, her feet ached, and she was beginning to wonder if she had taken on more than she could handle.

Nic joined her at home a short time later, looking equally tuckered out. They turned in not long after and, although Millie was exhausted, her mind refused to shut down.

A little niggling kept reminding her that regardless of what happened at the top of

Brimstone Hill between Danielle and Emilio, there was still someone on board the ship trying to get their hands on her suitcase.

Chapter 14

Millie woke early the next morning and flew through the second straight sea day, so wrapped up in keeping passengers entertained she barely had time to think about St. Kitts. Unfortunately, she more than made up for it that night, tossing and turning, worrying about Danielle not only meeting up with Emilio but also dealing with the emotions and memories it brought with it.

Nic had already left the apartment since he needed to be on the bridge when the harbor pilot boarded to help maneuver the massive cruise ship into Port Zante, St. Kitts' cruise port.

The ship shuddered, which meant they were close to docking. She poured a cup of coffee and followed Scout onto the balcony for her first glimpse of the port.

Like many other Caribbean islands *Siren of the Seas* visited, she could see colorful buildings in hues of bright red and gold. Pastels alongside vibrant shades. She breathed deeply, watching as the dock workers stood by, waiting to secure the ship.

Millie shifted her gaze and glimpsed Nic and a man clad in khaki, the harbor pilot, if she had to guess, standing on the outboard bridge wing.

The morning was shaping up to be sunny and warm...perfect weather for a hilltop excursion.

She finished her coffee, showered and changed into her work uniform. On her way out, she grabbed an apple and a container of Greek yogurt.

Millie reached her office and settled in at her desk. She had just enough time to go over the day's schedule before the entertainment staff arrived for their early morning meeting.

During the meeting, she handled a few minor issues, and the staff members who would remain on board to entertain the passengers were the first to leave.

Danielle lingered, waiting until the room cleared. Patterson arrived a short time later. "Are you ready to make the call?"

"I am." Danielle turned her cell phone on. "Crud. I'm not getting good reception down here."

"Let's head to the outdoor crew area."

The trio made the short trek to the other side of the ship and the crewmember's outdoor lounge and hot tub area.

Millie silently prayed as she watched Danielle tap the top of her phone. "Hello, Emilio. It's Danielle. I'm on a tight schedule and will have to meet you this morning at eleven. Call me back."

Danielle ended the call. "He didn't answer."

Ting.

Danielle's cell phone chirped. "It's him. He wants to meet me at a place called Black Rocks."

"That won't work," Patterson said. "I've already contacted the island's authorities. We're meeting at the top of Brimstone Hill National Fortress, agreeing it's the most remote spot with the least potential to have innocent bystanders become involved."

Millie couldn't resist. "Which is what I tried to tell you in the first place."

Patterson gave her a pointed stare but didn't reply.

"I'll let him know." Danielle grew quiet as she tapped out the message. "It needs to be Brimstone Hill at eleven."

Ting. "He doesn't seem to like that spot."

"Too bad. Tell him he either meets you at Brimstone Hill or he doesn't get the suitcase back."

Danielle's jaw tightened. "He must think I'm dumber than a box of rocks."

"No. I think he thinks you're desperate. Desperate to get your brother's belongings." Millie had a sudden thought. "Do you think he suspects it's some sort of trap?"

"Your guess is as good as mine. I don't know Emilio very well, only the few times I saw him years ago and what Casey told me." Danielle sent another text, asking for confirmation. "He's not replying."

"I say we move forward on the assumption he shows," Patterson said. "Are you still planning on taking the tour, Millie?"

"I am, along with Felix, Isla, Joy, Cat and Annette."

Patterson made an unhappy sound. "What is this...Millie's excursion adventure for crewmembers only?"

"No." Millie grinned. "It was Isla's idea. I invited Annette and didn't want to leave Cat out. Isla invited Joy and Felix. The excursion is full."

"Full of trouble."

173

Millie could tell Patterson was less than thrilled, but there wasn't much he could do. "You worry too much."

"Yeah. I worry about a drug deal going bad, the safety of the ship's crewmembers, not to mention being at the mercy of the local authorities."

"It'll be fine." Millie motioned to Danielle. "I haven't asked yet, but what exactly does Emilio look like?"

"He has...had dark hair, is about six inches taller than me and on the thin side, although I haven't seen him in a few years, so I have no idea what he looks like now."

A flurry of activity near the ship caught Millie's eye. It was the port workers sliding the gangway into place. "I need to see the first round of passengers off. I'll meet you at the end of the dock at nine, Danielle."

"See you then."

Millie hurried off and could feel Patterson's eyes following her. The head of security wasn't thrilled about a vanload of crewmembers being on hand during a potential drug bust.

But then, it was better than having a vanload of unsuspecting passengers. At least Annette, Danielle, Millie and even Cat had some experience in apprehending bad guys.

She was on the fence about Joy, having heard rumors about her possible involvement as a spy while living in the UK. Felix was a wildcard, but always up for an adventure.

Whatever happened, Millie was almost certain the trip to Brimstone Hill would eliminate one of the two people who were after the cocaine. Tracking down the crewmember would be phase two of the takedown operation.

*****

"Where's Danielle?" Millie began counting heads. Isla, Joy, Cat, Annette, and Felix were all there. The only one missing was the person they needed most, the person who was supposed to meet with Emilio.

She shaded her eyes and watched as passengers exited the ship, searching for blond hair and a thin frame. "She's never late."

"I see her." Felix, who was a head taller than the women, pointed her out.

Danielle emerged from the sea of people, moving at a quick pace and dragging a black suitcase behind her. "Sorry I'm late. Patterson and I were going over what he wants me to say." She patted her pocket. "I need to get a verbal confession about his involvement. He was also trying to coordinate with the island authorities."

"I hope they plan to beat us there," Annette said. "It's going to look awfully suspicious if a slew of uniformed officers show up after we get there."

"He's on his way. Brody is with him. He and the other ship's security are en route."

"Good." Millie dusted her hands. "Let's head to the van. Isla, this is your excursion. Lead the way."

Isla led them through the security checkpoint, passing by the welcome center, a bright yellow-orange building sporting a red metal roof, and turned right. The group zig zagged through another set of gates until they reached a gravel parking lot.

A section of the chain-link fence was missing and thick weeds crept up the sides. A dog ran toward them barking and snarling, only to be called back by a man wearing a tattered t-shirt, baggy shorts and dollar store flip flops.

"Sorry about my dog. You guys lost?"

"I...uh." Isla fumbled inside her pocket. "We were supposed to meet Desmond for a tour."

"Desmond Wattley?" The toothless man asked.

"He...uh... Yes. Desmond Wattley," Isla said. "I have his cell phone number. Maybe I should call him."

A cloud of dust appeared as a silver van sped toward them. The driver circled around and came to a stop a few feet away. A stocky man with dark curly hair, wearing a tan uniform hopped out. "Good morning, everyone. I am sorry if I'm late."

Isla stepped forward. "Desmond?"

The young man took a bow. "Yes, ma'am. Desmond Wattley at your service. You must be Isla."

"I am."

"And these people are with you?" Desmond smiled widely, dazzling them with his pearly whites.

"They are." Isla briefly introduced the group. "We're ready for our tour of Brimstone Hill."

"Brimstone Hill but first, Romney Manor."

"Romney Manor," Isla repeated. "Yes, the other part of our tour."

"We will visit Romney Manor first and then Brimstone Hill, which opens after ten."

"Any time before eleven would be perfect," Millie said. "What is Romney Manor?"

"I'm glad you asked." Desmond slid the van's side door open, placed a small footstool in front of it and began helping them inside. "Home to Caribelle Batik."

"Caribelle Batik?" Cat let out a squeal. "You're kidding?"

Millie scooched in next to Cat leaving enough room for Annette to fit on the other side. "What is Caribelle Batik?"

"Batik is patterned cloth using colored dye and wax. Caribelle Batik is considered to be some of the finest because they use sea island cotton. The colors are vibrant...absolutely gorgeous. Wait until you see the pieces," Cat said. "I could spend a small fortune on it."

"Would it be wedding-gown worthy?" Millie asked.

Cat had not yet picked out a wedding dress, insisting she wanted something casual, fitting the theme of a casual wedding.

"It would." Cat's eyes shined. "All my besties are here. It would be the perfect time to find a dress."

"Dress shopping it is," Joy said. "Will we be able to fit it in and still make it to Brimstone Hill before eleven?"

"You will need to shop quickly. We are on a bit of a tight schedule." Desmond helped Danielle, the last in line. "You have a suitcase."

"Yes. Uh. I hope it's not a problem."

"No problem," Desmond said. "Would you like me to put it in the storage area in the back?"

"If you don't mind."

"Not at all, lovely lady." While Felix climbed into the front passenger seat, Desmond grabbed the stool and carried that, along with the suitcase, to the back of the van.

He placed both inside before circling around to the driver's seat. "You will have forty-five minutes to explore Romney Manor and purchase Caribelle Batik items before we drive to Brimstone Hill."

"And you're sure we can be at Brimstone Hill before eleven?" Annette asked.

"One hundred percent. It is a drive across the island, but no worries. I pride myself on being punctual." Desmond spun the van in a tight circle, whipping around so fast, Millie's head hit the window.

He stomped on the gas pedal, and they tore out of the gravel parking lot.

The man and his dog stumbled back behind the dilapidated gate, which was nearly clipped by the van's rear bumper.

Something told Millie they were in for a wild ride.

Chapter 15

"I noticed you are all wearing the same ship lanyards and are members of the cruise ship's crew," Desmond said. "What do ya do?"

"I'm in charge of shore excursions," Isla said. "Most of the others work in the entertainment department except for Annette, who runs the ship's main galley."

"In charge of the food."

"Right," Annette confirmed.

"Then you would be my favorite lady," Desmond joked. "And what about you lovely blond-haired lady?"

"Danielle?" Isla nudged her.

"I...uh...also work in the entertainment department."

"As assistant cruise director," Millie added.

Desmond caught her eye in the rearview mirror, causing the van to wander toward the edge of the road.

"The road!" Millie shouted.

"We are all right." Desmond jerked the wheel and steered their van back onto the road. "For those of you who have never visited St. Kitts, we're called Kittitians, while our neighbors who live on Nevis are called Nevisians."

Their tour guide / driver careened left to pass a slow-moving truck. As luck would have it, a car was in the other lane, coming right toward them.

Millie squeezed her eyes shut and began praying. The van made a sudden turn. Her eyes flew open. She discovered they had veered off the main road and were speeding up a steep hill.

"Now that we've added dress shopping to the list, I'm taking a shortcut so we can arrive a little sooner." To prove his point, Desmond hit the gas, and they flew down the side road, making two fast turns and beating out a long line of traffic funneling in from the main road.

Desmond wove in and out of the lane, passing any vehicle driving below his desired speed.

Millie breathed a sigh of relief when they turned off. Her relief was short-lived when they began making their way along a narrow gravel road, inching higher and higher.

She cautiously peered out the window and instantly regretted her decision. The road dropped off on one side, with clumps of thick vegetation dotting the hilly terrain.

"Romney Manor and the adjoining Wingfield Estate have only had five owners. The first was Sam Jefferson. Jefferson was the great, great, great grandfather of Thomas Jefferson. He purchased the property in 1625." Desmond took his eyes off the narrow road, glancing at Danielle again in the rearview mirror, and the van drifted toward the edge of the cliff.

He quickly steered it back toward the center, sending loose rocks tumbling down the steep hill.

Millie pressed a hand to her chest, tearing her eyes away from the window. She forced herself to focus on Desmond's history lesson and not the fact that one slip of the wheel and they would tumble down the hill too.

"The property grew and distilled sugar cane for 350 years, until 2002, when it became an active archaeological site," Desmond explained. "The Duke of Edinburgh aka Prince Phillip visited in 1993."

"How exciting," Joy gasped.

"All I remember about his visit is the officials closed the roads so he could travel to Romney Manor."

They rounded a bend. The trees cleared and Millie could see lush green grass, a sea of pink, purple, yellow and blue flowers and gardens, along with several long, low buildings.

"We've arrived."

"Thank the Good Lord." Cat fumbled with her seatbelt. "I thought we were gonna drive over the cliff."

"You and me both," Annette muttered under her breath.

Desmond pulled between two other tour vans. He ran around the side and assisted the women, lingering longest when it was Danielle's turn. "Perhaps I could give you a personal tour."

"Thank you for the offer." Joy grasped Danielle's arm and propelled her away from Desmond. "I think we can manage on our own."

Felix waited until they were on the path leading to the main building and a safe distance away from their driver. "Maybe Danielle needs to sit up front, so that Desmond will only have to shift his gaze to the side to gawk at her."

Danielle shivered involuntarily. "He seems like a nice enough guy, but I don't want to be alone with him, if you know what I mean."

"Although you could easily give him a one, two karate chop and nip his special attention in the bud," Annette joked.

"Why does it always have to be me?"

"Because you're adorbs," Felix teased. "He seems to have a crush on you."

"I'm going to skip wandering around the grounds and start looking for a wedding dress," Cat said. "I'll catch up with you inside. By then, I should have a few contenders picked out."

"Not yet." Felix stopped her, motioning to a set of steps leading to a stone bell tower. "I see a super creepy bell tower up ahead. Let's get a group photo first."

"Who's going to take the picture?" Cat asked.

"Millie Armati?" A young woman with bright red hair began waving her arms and bustling toward them.

"Hello, Tara." Millie greeted the woman, one of the ship's passengers. "Are you enjoying your tour?"

"Yes, ma'am. This place is spectacular."

"C'mon, Millie." Joy motioned her over. "We need to hustle."

Millie held up her cell phone. "Would you mind taking our picture?"

"Not at all."

Millie handed Tara the phone and hurried up the steps to join her friends. She slipped in front of them and scooched down.

"You need to squeeze in a little closer," Tara said. "The woman on the right is getting cut out."

The group squeezed in even closer.

"I think I have it. Let me snap one more."

"I'm...getting a cramp in my foot," Isla groaned.

"Spider!" Cat scrambled out of the bell tower, fluffing her hair and stomping her feet. "Big, black hairy spider!"

Millie was close behind, with Danielle, Isla, Joy and Annette hot on her heels. "Thank you." She thanked Tara for taking the picture.

"Is there really a spider?" Tara's eyes were round as saucers. "I hate spiders."

Felix sauntered down the steps and caught up with them. "Scaredy cats. It was only a baby tarantula."

"Tarantula? That does it. I've had enough nature. I'm going inside to find a dress." Cat took off toward a sign marked *Caribelle Batik*.

"Did you really see a tarantula?" Danielle wrinkled her nose.

"I can't be sure, but it was a big, hairy spider." Felix ran his fingers up Danielle's arm.

She jerked away. "Very funny."

Felix craned his neck. "Before we head in for Cat's fashion show, I want to see the saman tree."

"The what tree?" Joy asked.

"Saman," Isla said. "It's the largest living organism in St. Kitts. The tree is four hundred years old and covers over half an acre."

"I see it." Millie circled around the gardens and stopped beneath a large tree, branching out in different directions, offering shade from the scorching sun.

"It's beautiful." Isla snapped a picture.

"It reminds me of a live oak," Annette said.

"It does." Millie ran a light hand over the trunk. "Four hundred years. This tree has seen a lot."

The group toured the grounds and caught up with Cat inside the store.

"Were you able to find anything?" Millie asked.

"I was," Cat beamed. "I have it narrowed down to two."

"Try them on," Felix chanted. "Try them on."

"I'll be right back." Cat dashed into the dressing room and emerged a short time later sporting a golden orange and yellow dress that crisscrossed around her neck, hugging her hips and legs. She spun in a slow circle. "Well?"

"I give it an eight," Felix said.

"I agree," Danielle said. "It's an eight."

"Seven point five," Isla said.

"I'm gonna go with a seven," Joy said.

"What about you Annette? Millie?"

"It's cute, but for me, the color seems a little off," Annette said. "On a one through ten, I'm gonna have to go with seven, although it fits you like a glove."

"Millie?" Cat asked.

"Eight because of your natural glow," Millie said. "Try the other one on."

Cat closed the curtain and must've been on a mission to set a record for quick changes because she was back in a flash, sporting a vibrant turquoise dress with pops of red and yellow.

Danielle let out a wolf whistle. "That's the dress."

"I agree," Millie said. "It's beautiful. The color compliments your hair and eyes."

"It reminds me of a bright, beautiful rainbow." Felix gave her a thumbs up. "You're going to knock Andy's socks off. This one is definitely a ten."

"Ten for me too," Millie said. "It's not too casual, not too formal."

"And the perfect length," Isla added. "Ten."

Joy and Annette voted with tens, giving Cat a solid seal of approval.

"This is the dress," she beamed.

"Break out the champagne," Joy joked. "We found the dress."

Cat returned to the changing room, and when she emerged moments later, she was glowing. "Thanks, guys. This is the best day ever. I love the dress. It's unique, original and something I'll treasure forever."

"Nothing like shopping with your besties," Felix said. "By the way, who is walking you down the aisle?"

Cat's eyes widened. "Walking me down the aisle?"

"You know." Felix began humming. "Here comes the bride."

"No one. I mean, you're my family."

"Mmm. Hmm." Felix arched a brow.

"Would you...like to walk me down the aisle?"

"I thought you would never ask." Felix impulsively hugged her. "I would be honored."

"Woo-hoo!" Millie hooted. "It's time to celebrate."

The clerk carefully wrapped Cat's wedding dress in tissue paper, and placed it inside a cream-colored box. "Congratulations on your upcoming wedding."

"Thank you."

"After watching you with your friends, I almost wish I could be there," she said. "You'll be a beautiful bride."

Cat strolled out of the shop on cloud nine, clutching her special purchase. They returned to find Desmond standing next to the van, waiting for them. "Well? Did you enjoy Romney Manor?"

"It was breathtaking," Millie said. "The views, the saman."

"The bell tower," Felix chuckled.

"Big, hairy spiders," Annette chimed in.

"We have a lot of nature on the island." Desmond slid the door open and helped the women back inside.

While Desmond wasn't looking, Felix motioned for Danielle to take the passenger seat, to which she stubbornly shook her head and scooted inside before he suggested it to their driver.

Millie was second to the last in and returned to her spot, sandwiched in between Annette and Cat. She fumbled for the seatbelt and snapped it in place, tugging on it as Desmond began backing out of the parking spot.

He hit the gas, and the van lurched forward, whipping Millie's head back.

"The drive to Romney Manor was easy. The trip to Brimstone Hill is trickier," Desmond warned. "If you are prone to motion sickness, I would prepare for it now. It can be a rough ride."

A collective groan went up and Millie was seriously beginning to regret suggesting Brimstone Hill as the meeting spot for Danielle and Emilio.

In fact, she was beginning to wonder if they would make it back to the ship in one piece.

Chapter 16

"This is it," Desmond announced while turning onto a side road. It immediately curved, giving the passengers a tiny taste of what was to come.

A narrow stone arch appeared, so narrow Millie was certain there was no way the van would make it through. She wasn't the only one.

"We're driving through there?" Felix gasped.

"We are. It's a tight fit."

"No kidding."

Desmond slowly inched forward and then promptly backed up. He pulled forward and backed up again, shifting the van ever so slightly each time. "I think we can make it now. Keep your fingers crossed we don't crunch."

Millie watched in awe as the van squeezed through the arch, clearing it on each side by what couldn't have been more than an inch.

After clearing the arch, the passengers broke out in spontaneous applause.

"You've done this a time or two," Isla said.

"Yes, ma'am. My first few tries weren't so smooth," Desmond said. "Now for the fun part."

The gravel road zigged and zagged, back and forth, back and forth, all the while climbing higher and higher.

"What a gorgeous view." Annette elbowed Millie. "Check it out."

"No thanks. I'm too busy turning green," Millie moaned.

"I didn't know you were prone to motion sickness." Cat patted her leg. "We should've brought some barf bags with us. Do you want to trade places in case you need to throw up out the window?"

"There will be no throwing up inside the van," Desmond said. "If you feel imminently ill, let me know and I'll stop in the road."

"Maybe you should move closer to the door." Joy reached for her seatbelt. "Would you like to trade places, Millie?"

"I'm not going to throw up. At least, I don't think so. I'll be fine." Millie motioned to Cat. "Maybe a little fresh air will help."

Her friend promptly slid the window open. "Seriously, let's trade places." She handed her box and dress to Annette and swapped places with Millie.

"Thanks, Cat."

"You're welcome, and if you feel sick, lean this way," she whispered.

"I promise...I'm not going to puke," Millie whispered back.

"The British were behind the construction of Brimstone Hill National Fortress. It was finally completed in the late 1700s. The fortress is a well-preserved example of British military architecture with stunning views of not only St. Kitts but also neighboring Nevis."

They continued climbing higher and higher, and Millie had to admit the views were spectacular.

"I will stop talking now and concentrate. The rest of the drive can be a little tricky." Desmond grew quiet, focusing his attention on the twisting, turning road. Although it didn't seem as "cliffy" as Romney Manor, it was still somewhat of a treacherous journey, and Millie was glad she wasn't the one behind the wheel.

Finally, the road leveled out, and it was a straight shot to the top. It opened onto a plateau. The fort was to the left with some outbuildings on the other side of a sea of green grass overlooking the water.

Desmond circled around and pulled alongside another tour van. "I will drop you off here. We are in van number seven. Don't forget it."

He ran around to assist the passengers, lingering a little longer when he got to Danielle. "Would you like a tour of Brimstone Hill?"

"I...uh...need to stick with my friends, but thank you for the generous offer." Danielle hurriedly stepped aside and began walking away.

Millie grabbed her arm. "The suitcase. Emilio. Why we're here."

"Right." Danielle motioned to Desmond. "I'll need my suitcase."

"Suitcase?" Desmond's brows furrowed. "How many souvenirs do you plan to buy?"

"I'm not sure yet. I have a...very large family," she fibbed.

Their tour guide shot her a puzzled look as he removed the black suitcase with the green and white cloth and handed it to her. "There are many steps to get to the Citadel, also known as Fort George."

Danielle wrinkled her nose. "The Citadel?"

"It is worth the climb. Are you sure you don't want me to go with you? I can carry your suitcase."

"That's very kind of you, but I can manage." Danielle hastily walked away before Desmond could offer additional assistance.

She caught up with the others. "He thinks I'm nuts," she said in a low voice. "Now what?"

"You go off on your own." Millie shot a furtive glance over her shoulder. "We don't want to spook Emilio. He could be watching us."

"Right. I wonder if Brody, Patterson and the others are here."

Annette casually looked around. "Over at twelve o'clock. Patterson is standing near the gift shop.

Brody is at the bottom of the stairs and I'm pretty sure I see Oscar standing near the cannon."

"You've got this," Millie said. "All you have to do is collect your brother's stuff, try to get him to admit to what's in the suitcase and walk away."

"The recorder is ready." Danielle patted her pocket. "I'll never be so happy to get rid of excess baggage." With a look of determination, she lifted the almost empty suitcase and carried it across the parking lot to the steps.

"Me and my bright ideas," Millie sighed.

"You were right about there only being one way in and one way out." Annette shaded her eyes, watching as Danielle began her ascent. "We should keep an eye on her."

"From a distance," Joy said. "We don't want it to appear that we're with her."

The group trekked after Danielle, climbing the long and low steps, which seemed to go on forever. Millie's hip started to ache, and she was seriously beginning to wonder what on earth she'd been thinking when they finally reached the top.

"It's gorgeous," Isla breathed. "The brochures don't do this place justice."

"And well-worth the harrowing journey," Cat said as she slipped her sunglasses on. "This would make a beautiful spot for a wedding."

"If we made it back up here in one piece," Joy joked.

"True. Maybe we'll appreciate it together and Andy and I will stick with our plan to exchange our vows on the helipad."

"I like that idea." Millie wandered around, keeping one eye on Danielle, who was slowly circling the Citadel's perimeter.

A familiar figure appeared at the top of the stairs. It was Patterson, clad in cargo shorts, a collared polo shirt and black tennis shoes. He casually shoved his hands in his pockets and strolled in Danielle's direction.

Millie shifted her gaze. Brody was close behind, a pair of binoculars in hand and a travel brochure sticking out of his front pocket.

"Let's keep moving," Annette said. "Do we have a description of Emilio?"

"Dark hair, about half a foot taller than Danielle and on the thin side," Millie said.

"Which fits the description of about a quarter of the men up here," Felix said.

"True. All we can do is keep an eye on her," Joy said.

"Maybe we should split up," Isla suggested. "We'll cover more ground."

Annette, Cat and Millie hung out a short distance from Danielle while Felix, Isla and Joy made a beeline for a wooden bridge. Crossing over a dry moat they disappeared from sight.

The sun was high in the sky, and beads of sweat formed on Millie's forehead. She checked her watch. Danielle had told Emilio she would meet him at eleven. Although he had never confirmed, surely he'd gotten her text, unless he'd lost signal and it never went through.

A half hour passed, and then forty-five minutes. Eleven o'clock came and went. Soon it would be time to return to the van and head back to the ship.

"I don't think he's gonna show," Cat said.

"Maybe he got spooked." Annette squinted her eyes and studied their surroundings.

An uneasiness settled over Millie. Something was wrong.

Danielle, who had stayed close to the stairs, caught Millie's eye. She gave a small shake of her head and began dragging the now dusty black suitcase to the bottom.

Patterson appeared and followed behind.

Giving them an ample head start, the rest of the group made their way down the steps. They caught up with Danielle, who was standing next to Desmond and the van.

"You are right on time." Desmond reached for Danielle's suitcase, a look of surprise on his face when he picked it up. "You didn't fill your suitcase with souvenirs?"

"I...uh. I ran out of time. There was so much to see." Danielle forced a laugh. "I guess I should have left it on the ship."

Desmond shot her an odd look as he placed the suitcase in the back of the van, muttering under his breath about women and shopping.

Cat tightened the strap on her wide-brimmed straw hat and followed their tour guide. "I noticed a spot called monkey hill. I read somewhere that the island is full of wild monkeys."

"Nearly sixty thousand was the last count I heard," Desmond said.

Felix made a choking sound. "Sixty thousand monkeys?"

"There are almost fifty thousand islanders in St. Kitts and Nevis combined, which means there are more monkeys than people," he said. "They are a menace. You may think they are cute, but they are nothing but trouble."

"I thought islanders kept them as pets and they were tame."

"They keep them as tourist attractions, so you will pay money to take pictures."

"Which is what I'm hoping to do," Cat said. "Get a picture, that is."

"They are also little thieves who come down into town at night and steal whatever they can."

"I've never seen a monkey in the wild. I could've sworn I saw some when I was up in the Citadel. Give me a couple of minutes. I'll be right back." Cat circled around the side of the van and hurried toward a grassy parking area off to the side. She climbed on a low stone wall and pulled her cell phone from her pocket.

Millie thought she saw something moving in the tall grass. A dark face with tufts of light-colored fur appeared mere feet from where Cat stood.

"It's one of the furry beasts. He's got your friend in his sights!" Desmond made a move to warn Cat. It was too late. The monkey scampered across the wall and latched onto her leg.

She let out an ear-piercing scream before tumbling over the side and disappearing.

Chapter 17

Millie took off at a dead run toward the low wall Cat had fallen from after being attacked by a monkey.

Desmond quickly caught up with her and ran ahead. He vaulted over the stone wall, and Millie could see him bending down.

She wasn't agile enough to vault but managed a respectable scramble to the other side, where she found Cat flat on her back, clutching her cell phone and staring up at the bright blue skies. "I felt something with sharp nails grabbing my leg. What was it?"

"One of those cute as a button monkeys you wanted to take a picture of. Are you all right?"

"Yeah. Although it scared me half to death."

Desmond helped Cat to her feet. "They are clever fellows, always on the prowl to steal something. You're lucky he didn't get your cell phone."

Cat's eyes grew round as saucers as she patted her hat. "They're gone."

"What's gone?"

"My sunglasses." She began feeling around. "I had them on top of my hat."

Whoo, hoo.

"They must've fallen off, and the sneaky thief took them." Desmond jabbed his finger toward a clump of bushes about fifteen feet away, where a monkey sat watching them, twirling Cat's sunglasses.

"He has my sunglasses." Cat started to go after him.

Desmond stopped her. "You do not want to fight the monkey for your sunglasses. You won't win."

The bushes moved, and several more monkeys appeared, curiously watching Cat, Desmond, and Millie.

"We're outnumbered."

"Here's your chance to get a great photo of them," Millie joked.

"Haha." Cat snapped a picture. "I love those sunglasses and paid a pretty penny for them." She dusted off her Bermuda shorts and climbed over the low wall.

Millie followed behind, with Desmond bringing up the rear, keeping a close eye on the monkeys. "At least you weren't hurt."

"It could have been much worse," Desmond said. "They bite hard and carry diseases."

With the crisis averted, the trio caught up with the others.

"What happened?" Danielle asked as soon as they were inside. "It looked like a monkey attacked Cat."

"He stole my sunglasses."

"But she got a great shot of a bunch of them in the wild." Millie climbed in the van. "You should've seen the look on your face when you saw the monkey holding your sunglasses."

"I paid fifty bucks for my Shady Rays," Cat said glumly.

"Other than the run-in with the monkey menace, did you enjoy Brimstone Hill?" Desmond asked.

"Immensely," Isla said. "I would highly recommend this tour and you to any of our passengers."

"Thank you, Isla. I enjoy my job." Desmond tapped the brakes as the van began making its descent. They crossed paths with another tour van, this one making its way up the hill. He eased off to the side, giving them just enough room to pass.

"What happens if we run into a van on the way down?"

"Then we will have troubles," Desmond said. "It happens every once in a while, but not too often. I know the other drivers' schedules as they do mine. There is only one spot going down where there is room to pull over. It's the private vehicles that present a problem."

Millie refused to look out the window. Instead, she began flipping through the pictures she'd taken of Romney Manor and the saman tree. She chuckled when she found the photo of all of them crammed in the bell tower and the next picture of Cat running out, screaming after the spider scare.

"Check it out, Cat." She handed the phone to her friend. "The look on your face is priceless. First the spider scare and then the monkey."

"Ugh." She rolled her eyes. "I'm beginning to think there's way too much nature on this island. Delete that."

"No way." Millie snatched her phone back. "I think it's great."

A car flew around the hairpin turn, and Desmond jerked the wheel.

Thunk. The van's front tire hit something hard, hard enough to jar the occupants.

Felix craned his neck. "You hit a large rock."

"Pete the puncturer," Desmond said. "The rock has been known to take out a tire or two."

The van continued inching down the incline, but as they progressed, they began jostling up and down.

"We're on some uneven terrain," Joy said.

"Not quite," their driver grimaced. "I believe Pete the puncturer gave us a flat. Remember the spot I mentioned? It's up ahead. I'll pull off to check the damage."

The group grew quiet while Desmond steered the van to the level spot, as far off the road as possible.

"I will be right back." He climbed out and tromped around the front. His expression grew grimmer as he stared at the front of the van.

"See if we have a flat, Felix," Annette said.

"I'm gonna bet ten bucks we do," Isla said. "That was a big bump."

Felix unbuckled and exited the van.

Millie could see the men talking, looking from the front of the van to the back.

They trudged around the side and Desmond opened the rear cargo door. "We have a flat. Felix and I should have it fixed quickly, but you will have to get out."

The women exited single file and hovered near the back, careful to stay out of the traffic lane.

"The heat is brutal out here." Joy swatted at a fly. "I don't think I would enjoy living in the Caribbean."

"You pretty much do," Millie pointed out.

"With one major difference. Those ocean breezes, not to mention air conditioning, make it much more bearable."

Annette grabbed her travel brochure and began fanning her face. "This is a gentle reminder of how blessed we are."

"Thanks for coming with me, guys," Danielle said. "I'm sorry it was a bust. I was so sure Emilio would show."

"Me too," Millie said. "We're back to square one."

Isla dabbed at her forehead. "I'm going to grab my bottled water." She squeezed around the side and slid the door open.

Millie could see her sipping her water. She set it down and slid the door shut.

"I could use some water, too." Cat began following behind when she suddenly froze. She let out a half squeal and stumbled back.

Thinking she'd seen another spider or worse...a venomous snake, Millie began scrambling around, trying to find a stick or some other sort of weapon.

"What is it?" Danielle bolted past Millie and rushed to Cat's side. She stopped dead in her tracks. "What the..."

Millie ran toward them, gripping the stick she'd found, preparing to battle whatever rodent, reptile, or arachnid she might encounter.

Instead, she saw a shoe...and a leg sticking out of the bushes.

"Desmond, Felix!" Danielle began frantically motioning to them. "There's someone over here."

Desmond dropped the tire jack and joined them. "Who is it?"

"Someone is in the bushes."

Felix caught up. "What's going on?"

"We found a body in the bushes," Cat said.

Desmond surveyed the area. "The van is too close. I need to move it away." He cautiously made his way back inside and eased the van forward. He returned and motioned for Felix to grab one leg while he grabbed the other.

The women huddled together, watching in horror as they pulled the man, clad in jeans and a lightweight cotton shirt, out into the open.

Danielle's face turned ghostly white. "Emilio."

Chapter 18

Millie could feel the blood drain from her face. "This is Emilio?"

"Yes."

"Who is Emilio?" Desmond asked.

"A...friend who recently moved to St. Kitts. Is he..."

Their tour guide knelt next to the body and touched the side of his neck. "He is not alive." He reached into his pants pocket. "I will call the Royal St. Christopher."

"Royal St. Christopher?" Annette asked. "Shouldn't you call the police?"

"That is our police." Desmond placed the call, explained the situation, and gave the operator their exact location. "They are on the way." He inched closer. "This man looks familiar. I've seen him around."

Millie blinked rapidly. "You recognize Emilio?"

"Yes. At the port, when the cruise ships are arriving and I'm waiting for my tour group. He has a vendor booth and sells merchandise. We have a lot of local artists who sell goods."

"What kind of stuff was he selling?" Millie asked.

"Patriots merchandise," Desmond said. "St. Kitts and Nevis Patriots is the name of our cricket team."

Millie motioned to Danielle. "Show Desmond the surveillance video with the reflective emblem."

Danielle tracked down the video of the man wearing the jacket and showed it to Desmond. "Does your sports team have an emblem that looks like this?"

Desmond grew quiet, studying the video. "Yes. Although it is a little dark, it looks like one of our jackets. They are very popular."

A tour van rounded the corner and slowed, cautiously creeping past their disabled vehicle. Another vehicle was close behind.

"Patterson. We need to get Patterson down here," Danielle said. "I think he's still at the top."

"You're right." Millie grabbed her cell phone and dialed Patterson's number.

"Dave Patterson speaking. What's up Millie?"

"Our tour van is halfway down the hill. We found Emilio's body."

There was silence on the other end, lasting so long, Millie thought they'd been disconnected. "Are you still there?"

"I'm here."

"Did you hear me? Emilio is dead. Our van got a flat tire. We pulled off into the only grassy area available and that's when we found him."

"How far down the hill?" Millie could tell Patterson was on the move.

"You can't miss us. We're just past the second set of switchbacks."

"I'm on my way."

"We'll be here." Millie ended the call and waved her phone in the air. "Patterson should be here in a couple of minutes."

"Who is Patterson?" Desmond asked. "I've phoned the police."

"Dave Patterson is Siren of the Seas' head of security," Annette said. "He...we saw him up on the hill when we were having a look around."

"More of the ship's employees are here on a tour?" Desmond's jaw dropped. "Is there anyone left on board your ship?"

"Of course, there are crewmembers still on board," Annette said. "I say we move away from the body and let the authorities take over."

"I agree. We don't want to contaminate potential evidence." Millie clicked on her phone's camera icon, inched closer to the body, and snapped two pictures, each from a different angle.

Annette grabbed her arm. "I see a cop-looking car coming this way."

"Right." Millie hurriedly switched her cell phone off and slid it into her fanny pack.

A four-door sedan crept closer and pulled in directly behind their disabled van.

Patterson, Oscar, Brody, and the two men Millie had seen them talking with at the top emerged.

The ship's head of security was the first to catch up with them. "Where is he?"

"Over here." Desmond waited for the others to join them and then led them to the body.

The ship's security team and what Millie suspected were St. Kitts' authorities dressed in civilian clothing, had a brief discussion and returned to where the women and Felix, stood watching.

"We need you to tell us exactly what happened," Patterson said.

Taking turns, they filled them in on how they'd found Emilio's body.

"You just happened to pull over in this exact spot and found him." The officer who appeared to be in charge looked skeptical. And Millie couldn't blame him.

"I travel this way every day, sir," Desmond said. "There is only one pull-off area to and from the fort. This is it. If you were planning to get rid of someone, this would be the spot."

Patterson motioned to Danielle. "Can you confirm this man's identity?"

"I can. His name is Emilio Torres. He was an acquaintance. We were supposed to meet at the fort at eleven," Danielle said.

"Can you confirm your whereabouts during the last twenty-four hours?" the officer asked.

"I was on board Siren of the Seas until we docked this morning. I didn't exit the ship until almost nine. My keycard can confirm the time."

"Danielle has been with us from nine o'clock on," Millie added. "All of us."

The authorities asked a few more questions and then told them they could leave, but took Desmond's information to follow up. "You'll need to move the van."

"We're not going anywhere until I finish fixing the flat tire."

While the others worked on fixing the flat, Brody pulled Danielle aside and Millie could see they were having a serious conversation. Finally, they joined the others. Her friend's face was pale except for her cheeks, which were now bright red.

The men made quick work of swapping out the tire for the spare, and soon the group was on their way again.

Desmond grew quiet, concentrating on the drive down, until they reached the bottom. "You know the dead man."

"I knew him," Danielle said. "He was my brother's friend."

"Your brother is also here?"

"He died a few years ago."

"I'm sorry to hear that," Desmond said. "My condolences."

"Thank you."

"The suitcase. You were not filling it with souvenirs. You said you were meeting the man. Did you plan to give him the suitcase?"

"I was. He...did me a favor by sending me some important items and I was going to give his suitcase back to him."

"What was his name again?"

"Emilio Torres."

"Emilio Torres," Desmond repeated. "He must have been in trouble. I know many people on St. Kitts. They talk, you know. I might be able to find something out about him. As I mentioned, I'm almost certain he had a vendor booth down by the port."

Danielle clasped her hands. "That would be great."

"A lot of Kittitians work at the port. It's a small island, a small community. I am not the only one who knows who Emilio is. Strangers, they come here to work and live, but they don't stay strangers."

Millie leaned forward. "It would be wonderful if you could do a little digging around for us. We need to get back on board the ship. Danielle would be eternally grateful, wouldn't you, Danielle?" She nudged her friend, giving her the eye.

"Yes. I." Danielle's voice softened. "That would be so sweet of you, Desmond. I mean, I would be forever in your debt."

Desmond cast her a shy glance. "If you give me your cell phone number, I can call you if I find anything."

"I."

"She would love to," Millie blurted out.

Danielle reluctantly removed her cell phone from her pocket. "What's your cell phone number? I'll send you a text."

Desmond rattled off his number.

"Done."

"People talk, not always to the authorities, but to each other."

"What if we threw in some cash for your time?" Millie unzipped her fanny pack and removed her wallet. "I have fifty bucks."

Cat unzipped the front pocket of her backpack. "I have another twenty."

"I have fifty." Annette handed her money to Millie.

"Here's another twenty." Isla handed Millie some cash.

"I want to help." Joy handed Millie a ten, a five, and a stack of ones.

"We're in this together." Felix pulled some bills from his pocket and handed them to Millie.

She quickly counted out the cash. "We have over two hundred dollars for your tip and to put toward your investigative efforts on our behalf."

"Will you be returning to St. Kitts?" Desmond glanced in the rearview mirror.

"We'll be back," Millie said.

"I'm meeting with my friends as we prepare for our annual festival, the Sugar Mas." Desmond tapped the steering wheel, as if in deep thought.

Millie hoped he wasn't changing his mind about helping. "So, it won't take long."

"It should not take long at all." In Desmond fashion, they arrived back at the port in record time, passing several slower-moving vehicles along the way. "You are back, safe and sound."

"Except for finding a body," Joy reminded him.

"Something tells me we will find out swiftly what happened to your friend, Danielle."

"Acquaintance," she corrected. "Thank you, Desmond. I appreciate any help you can give me, can give us."

"You are welcome. Perhaps you will have time to meet me for lunch when you come back to St. Kitts," he hinted.

"You know it." Danielle gave him a thumbs up.

The others collected their belongings, including Cat's dress and Danielle's empty suitcase. With a promise to do some digging around, Desmond climbed back inside his van and drove off.

"Well?" Millie asked after he was gone. "Do you think he'll be able to help?"

"He's our best shot. If Emilio was fronting with a legit business here at the port, I'm almost certain he and Desmond crossed paths." Danielle sucked in a breath. "I hope he comes through and would be happy to buy him lunch but there's no way I'm meeting him alone."

Chapter 19

"We need to go over everything we have so far about Emilio's death while it's still fresh in our minds," Annette said. "Let's meet in my office."

"Also known as the galley," Joy said. "I like your idea. We did a lot of walking and stairs, and I'm getting kinda hungry."

"Yeah, finding a body always works up an appetite," Felix said sarcastically.

"I don't think Joy was suggesting that," Millie said. "A death would sadden any compassionate human being. Although the more we're learning, the more inclined I am to believe his death wasn't accidental or of natural causes."

"I'm with Millie," Cat said. "If what Desmond told us is true and Emilio was a vendor here at the port, he was using his business as a front to move illegal drugs in and out of the country."

"With the help of ship employees," Danielle added. "If you think about it, he'd have the perfect setup. Emilio had connections in the US. He moved here and set up shop in the Caribbean to transfer drugs from here to there or vice versa. All he needed were points of contact, employees from each of the ships that docked at the port. People with security clearance and access to restricted areas."

"And insider information about how to avoid detection," Joy said. "Now all we need to figure out is who Emilio's contact was on board our ship."

"Contact and potential killer," Annette said. "It's cooking out here. I'm ready to head inside."

Millie lingered while the others went on ahead, through the welcome center and past a cluster of vendors lining the sidewalks, all hawking their wares.

She slowed, noting the distance between the shopping district and the security checkpoint. It was only a few steps. If Emilio had set up a legit business, he was only steps away from the checkpoint and arriving ships.

There was a line to pass through security, giving Millie time to snap a few pictures of the area for future reference. She got caught behind a group of passengers re-boarding and finally caught up with her friends, who stood waiting for her on the other side.

"What happened to you?" Annette asked when she finally made it through.

"I was taking pictures of the vendors and the shopping area." Millie shoved her phone in her pack. "Let's head upstairs and start putting a timeline together, a potential list of suspects, and a plan to keep Danielle safe."

"Because if whoever took Emilio out is on board this ship, her life is in danger," Cat said. "This is terrible."

"Much worse than worrying about Danielle being on the hook for drug possession," Millie added.

The group climbed the crewmember's gangway, dinging their keycards and running personal items and purchases through the scanner.

Everyone made it through without incident. Everyone except for Danielle and the black suitcase.

Millie knew trouble was brewing when the woman in charge called Suharto, the head of gangway security, over. They talked in low voices, looking toward the group every couple of seconds.

"It's the bag," Danielle hissed. "I have no idea what Patterson put in there. Whatever it is, it's being flagged."

Suharto took the woman's place at the scanning station and ran the suitcase back and forth. Finally, he removed it from the conveyor belt and carried it over to where they stood waiting.

"Who does this suitcase belong to?" he asked.

"Patterson," Annette said.

"Dave Patterson?" Suharto's eyes widened.

"He gave it to Danielle this morning after we exited the ship," Millie explained.

Suharto appeared understandably confused. "Who brought it back on board?"

"I did." Danielle raised her hand. "Although I don't know what Patterson placed inside," she answered truthfully.

"Millie?" Suharto turned to Millie. "I'm not sure what's going on here, but something tells me you're involved."

Felix snickered, and Millie shot him a dark look. "What is that supposed to mean?"

A small group of crewmembers gathered nearby, whispering and watching the exchange.

"Let's discuss this where we won't have an audience." Suharto unhooked the bright yellow retractable belt used to direct crewmembers off the ship.

Millie and her entourage passed through single file, all cramming into the tight space used for storing contraband items before they were moved to the locked storage rooms.

She stepped inside, her heart hammering in her chest as her claustrophobia threatened to kick in.

Annette, noting her discomfort, cleared a spot to let her stand near the back. Meanwhile, Danielle moved to the front, watching as Suharto placed the suitcase on top of a small metal table. He unzipped both ends and flipped it open.

At first, the suitcase appeared empty until a gloved Suharto peeled back the lining and removed what appeared to be the block of cocaine.

Millie stared at it in disbelief. There was no way Patterson would have allowed the cocaine to leave the ship, let alone given it to Danielle.

"This appears to be an illegal substance," Suharto said. "I will have to test it."

"It's not cocaine," Millie said. "I would bet my life on it."

"We will see."

Danielle shrank back at the look of disappointment on Suharto's face. He gazed around the small room. "I hope you are right and I am wrong."

You could've heard a pin drop as he removed a small test kit, identical to the one Patterson had used to test the real deal, from the nearby cabinet.

Despite being almost one hundred percent certain Patterson had not planted the actual drug in the suitcase, Millie could feel a knot forming in the pit of her stomach.

Suharto carefully set the suitcase aside and when he lifted the brick, a flicker of surprise crossed his face. Millie thought she knew why. Whatever the white brick was, it didn't have the feel of the actual drug.

Her suspicions were confirmed when he unwrapped it and held it up for a closer inspection. Using a jackknife, he tried carving out a small sliver. Unlike the cocaine, he was having trouble obtaining a sample.

"At the risk of sounding like a broken record, this isn't cocaine," she said. "It's a plant, a fake drug."

Finally, Suharto was able to remove a small chunk. He placed it on top of a glass slide. Next, he opened a silver striped pouch with a cotton swab inside and rolled the swab across the small sample, twirling it back and forth several times.

He pressed the swab against a strip of paper which was also inside the packet and held it down.

"Please don't turn blue," Danielle whispered. "Patterson wouldn't do that to me."

"Think of all the paperwork this would create," Annette said. "It would be an internal nightmare."

It was only a matter of seconds before he lifted the swab. Millie nearly applauded when she saw the dull white strip and swab. The sample had tested negative for drugs.

Danielle's shoulders slumped, and she pressed a hand to her chest. "Whew. That was a close one."

"Close only counts in horseshoes and hand grenades," Joy joked. "Although, I have to admit, I was sweating bullets for a second there."

Suharto shook his head. "This can't be. Why would Patterson...why would you transport fake drugs in and out of the port?"

"It's a long story," Millie said. "Unfortunately, it involves Danielle being injured, us finding a body, and the possibility that someone on board this ship is a killer."

Suharto made a choking sound. "You're joking."

"I wish we were," Cat sighed.

"What is this?" Suharto lifted the clunky bar. It made a dull thud when he dropped it on the table.

Annette squeezed past Joy and Isla. "May I?"

"Be my guest." Suharto stepped away.

Annette borrowed his pocketknife and carved out a small piece. "This isn't even close to powder. Emilio wouldn't have been fooled for a minute."

"He didn't have to be fooled," Danielle said. "The only thing I had to do was get him to confess to what he'd sent me."

"Who is Emilio?" Suharto asked. "Never mind. I'm sure I don't want to know."

"Remember when I mentioned a body?" Millie asked. "We found Emilio, an acquaintance of Danielle's, dead on our way back from Brimstone Hill, an excursion we were on."

"We were conducting a sting," Felix said. "Emilio was supposed to meet her at the top of Brimstone Hill."

Isla picked up. "He didn't show. On the way down, our crazy tour guide / driver, Desmond, hit a big rock, and we got a flat tire."

"So we pulled off on the side of the road. While Felix and Desmond were fixing the flat, we found the body," Joy said.

"Stop." Suharto placed his hands on the side of his head, a pained expression on his face. "You are giving me a headache. How do these things happen?"

"To Millie?" Annette asked. "You know, as well as the rest of us, it's a fairly common occurrence."

"Bodies, drugs, out-of-control mechanical bulls," Cat said.

"Poisoned food, mafia kingpins killed in the ship's sauna," Isla added.

"Seriously, shouldn't we focus on the task at hand, which is figuring out what Patterson planted inside the suitcase?" Millie reminded them.

Danielle bounced on the tips of her toes. "I'm curious to know what it is."

"It might come in handy down the road, if we ever get involved in another drug sting," Joy said.

"Bite your tongue." Felix placed both hands on his hips. "Today's outing was exciting enough to last me a while."

"Then you had better stop hanging around Millie," Cat joked.

Millie frowned at her friend. "All I'm trying to do is help Danielle."

"We need to clear this up and head to the galley before we run out of time." Using the edge of her blouse, Annette cleaned the knife's blade and set it aside. She licked the tip of her finger and pressed it against the grainy substance before tasting it. "Just what I thought." She wrapped it back in plastic and held it up. "Mind if I take this with me?"

"Be my guest," Suharto said. "It's not a contraband item."

"What is it?" Cat and Joy asked in unison.

"A block of salt," Annette said. "And the next time Patterson borrows something from my kitchen, he needs to run it by me first."

Chapter 20

"Let's start with what we know." Millie took a blank piece of paper and pen from Annette's clipboard. "Emilio was selling merchandise near the port. He was also transporting drugs, possibly to and from the arriving ships."

"And someone on board our ship was working with him," Danielle said. "The deal went bad. Emilio was murdered. His killer is on the loose and could very well be employed by Majestic Cruise Lines."

Annette drummed her fingers on the counter. "We need a profile. Assuming you're correct and Emilio had a partner or partners on board cruise ships helping him send and receive drugs, we need to narrow down this partner / killer's profile."

"Good idea," Cat said.

"Desmond gave us one crucial clue," Joy said. "The St. Kitts & Nevis Patriots' jacket. If we can confirm the jackets Emilio sold match the one worn by whoever was digging through lost and found and also broke into Danielle's cabin, we can work on a description and a profile."

Annette set her laptop on the counter and logged in. Meanwhile, Danielle forwarded the videos. After finishing, the group gathered around, watching each clip.

"Can you play the lost and found one again?"

Annette rewound and hit play. They reached the point where the person turned and the reflective logo caught the light.

"Stop," Millie said.

Annette hit the pause button.

"I already have a printout of this at home but I don't want to waste time going back there. Can you print this?"

"Sure can." Annette tapped the keys. The printer on the desk behind them whirred and spit out a single sheet of paper. "Let me guess...you want another printout, this one of the person who kicked Danielle's door in."

"Yep."

Annette clicked out of the video, pulled up the other one and hit play. When they reached the part where the vandal appeared, she hit pause and then print.

Isla ran over to the printer, grabbed both sheets, and set them on the table. "Now what?"

"We track down the Patriots' logo to confirm we have a match."

"I'm on it." Annette opened a new search screen and typed in St. Kitts & Nevis Patriots. Several sites appeared. She double-clicked on the one at the top and a reflective green and red logo with splashes of black popped up.

"The spikes on the helmet," Cat gasped. "You can almost see spikes on the jacket."

Millie held the sheets of paper next to the computer screen. "Well?"

"It's a match, although it doesn't mean we have our guy...or gal." Danielle blew air through thinned lips. "We need to work on a profile."

Amit appeared, pushing a cart filled with RTG sack meals. "I thought I heard voices. How did it go?"

Joy gave Amit a thumbs down. "Not only were we unable to clear Danielle's name, the guy she was supposed to meet is dead."

"D-dead?" Amit stammered. "How did he die?"

"Good question, and one I hope we have an answer to soon," Millie said. "I snapped a couple pictures of Emilio's body. Unfortunately, there's not much to go on."

Felix eyed the bags on the cart. "What's in the bags?"

"Ready-to-go meals. Are you hungry?"

"Famished," Isla groaned. "I was so afraid I was going to be late for the excursion, I skipped breakfast."

"Ditto for me," Joy said. "Although I grabbed a banana from the buffet on my way downstairs."

"I will feed you." Amit hustled back and forth, passing out the bags of food while the group took turns washing their hands.

They gathered at the table while Amit added large bowls of coleslaw, pasta salad, and baked beans.

"Thank you, Amit," Millie said. "Would you like to join us?"

"Yes, if you don't mind. I haven't eaten. We were busy, even today, with the ship in port."

"Thanks for taking one for the team," Annette said. "You're the best."

Danielle lifted her glass. "Here's to Amit, the best galley assistant on the high seas."

They clinked glasses. Millie took a sip of water and set hers down. "I would like to say a special prayer for Danielle and Emilio's family."

The group bowed their heads as she began, "Dear Heavenly Father, we say a special prayer today for Danielle. Lord, you know she's still saddened by the death of her brother and was hoping to have small mementos of him returned to her, but it hasn't turned out that way."

Annette picked up. "We pray for Emilio Torres's family, that you bring them comfort in their time of grief. In our busy, chaotic world on board this ship, may we always be mindful you are the calm in our daily storms and our only hope for eternal life. Thank you for this food, for the friends gathered around this table, and for your help in figuring out who is now targeting Danielle. We thank you for our Savior, Jesus and in his name we pray, amen."

"Amen," the group echoed.

While they threw out scenarios about what may have happened to Emilio, they feasted on the salads and beans, soft tortillas stuffed with tender beef, shredded cheddar cheese, olives, onions, lettuce and tomatoes.

"The tortilla sauce is delish," Joy said. "What is it?"

"I was thinking the same thing," Cat plucked a piece of meat from her wrap. "It tastes like ranch, but with a hint of heat."

"It has a pinch of lime juice and hot sauce," Annette said. "We've been tinkering with new dressings. Do you like it?"

"Love it," Danielle said. "There are so many flavors—the olives and chopped red onion. It gives it a little zip."

"Good." Annette beamed. "I appreciate the feedback."

"The portion size is perfect. And these peanut butter cookies?" Felix rolled his eyes. "Are to die for."

"To die for?" Cat nudged him.

"I didn't mean literally."

"I know you didn't," she said. "But it reminds us why we're here."

"To come up with a killer profile." Balancing her wrap in one hand, Millie grabbed the pen and paper and began writing, *Drug Dealer / Possible Killer— Emilio Torres* at the top of the blank sheet and began adding what they knew:

Accomplice is a ship employee.

Works in crew maintenance.

Has access and clearance to cargo and cargo storage area, including lost and found.

Has knowledge of the timeline of when cargo and passengers' belongings are loaded and unloaded from the ship.

Has knowledge of when drug-sniffing dogs are brought into the cargo storage area.

Has been to St. Kitts before and possibly connected to Emilio Torres.

Annette stopped Millie. "I'm not sure the last one is a given. Think about it. It's possible the crewmember met Emilio *prior* to him moving here. Emilio had already traveled to St. Kitts, started his legitimate business operations and gave this person, him or her, the jacket."

"True," Millie agreed. "I'll add a question mark at the end." She added the question mark and then jotted down the last profile item.

Able to leave the ship as soon as it docked to meet Emilio.

Danielle polished off her wrap, hopped off the barstool, and peered over Millie's shoulder. "The last item is the key. If we can figure out which crewmembers left the ship as soon as it docked this morning, we can narrow down the list of potential suspects."

"I hate to gobble up my food and run, but I need to head upstairs for my boot stompin' boogie class." Felix tossed his paper bag and wrappers in the recycle bin and hugged Danielle. "Hang in there, girlfriend. We're gonna get to the bottom of this."

"Thanks, Felix. I'm sorry you got dragged into it," Danielle apologized.

"No need to apologize. I invited myself. I figured going anywhere with Millie would be an adventure, although I have to confess I wasn't prepared for today."

"I don't think any of us were." Cat slid off the stool. "I need to check in at the store."

"Toodles." Felix blew the rest of them a kiss.

Isla left with Felix, and Cat and Joy weren't far behind.

"Let me know if there's anything I can do to help," Joy said. "I'll be keeping my eyes and ears open and be on the lookout for the Patriots' jacket."

"Thanks, Joy," Danielle said. "I need all the help I can get."

Amit, Annette, Danielle, and Millie were the only ones left. They finished clearing the table, placing the leftovers back in the fridge.

"Hey." Danielle motioned to Millie. "What about the picture you took of Emilio's body?"

"I took two." Millie pulled them up on her cell phone and handed it to Danielle and Annette. "There isn't much to see."

"Judging by the condition of his body, he couldn't have been out there for very long, maybe a couple of hours," Annette theorized.

Millie bit the corner of her lower lip. "I keep thinking about this morning when you tried calling Emilio. You never actually talked to him."

"Correct."

"So perhaps you weren't communicating with Emilio but his killer who somehow found out about your meeting."

"True. He could have already been dead."

"It's a thought," Millie said. "It wouldn't have been difficult for the killer to confiscate his phone."

Amit peered over Annette's shoulder. His complexion turned a shade of green and he clutched his gut. "It is very sad."

"It is," Danielle agreed. "A small part of me always blamed Emilio for Casey's death, but it doesn't mean I wanted him dead."

Millie stared at her. "What did you say?"

"A part of me always blamed..." Danielle's voice trailed off. "I had a motive to kill Emilio, didn't I?"

Millie briefly closed her eyes. "Yes. Unfortunately, if the authorities find out about your relationship with Emilio, then you most definitely had a motive. It's a good thing you have an airtight alibi."

Chapter 21

Danielle's voice rose an octave. "I've been under Doctor Gundervan's care. He prescribed drugs for me when I was dealing with emotional issues related to Casey's death."

"It doesn't mean you're a killer."

"I could've hired someone to take him out." Danielle pressed a light hand to her forehead. "They could easily pin this on me. It's my word against a dead man's and dead men don't talk."

Millie could see panic setting in. She stepped in front of Danielle and grasped both her arms. "You didn't kill Emilio. Yes, there's still a concern about you being on the hook for the drugs because you can't prove they weren't yours."

"Unless we can figure out who is after them," Annette said. "That's our best bet."

"Not to mention we need to find this person. If someone murdered Emilio, Danielle might very well be the killer's next target."

"Could it get any worse?" Danielle sucked in a breath. "Yes. Yes, it could. The St. Kitts' authorities could haul me off to jail. I'll rot in a cockroach-infested, snake-infested jungle jail never to be seen again."

Millie gave her a gentle shake. "You're not going anywhere. Patterson knows you weren't responsible for Emilio's death. Yes, you left the ship, but you also have not one, not two, but six witnesses."

"Seven if you count Desmond," Annette said.

"Who is Desmond?" Amit interrupted.

"Our crazy tour guide who has a crush on Danielle," Millie said.

"I'm almost half-hoping he doesn't come up with anything, so I don't have to meet him for lunch," Danielle muttered.

"Danielle," Annette chided. "He was very nice."

"I think he's going to bend over backwards to help so he can see Danielle again," Millie predicted. "Although Brody might not be thrilled about you having lunch with the guy."

"Brody can go with me."

"Our most pressing concern is that there's potentially a killer on board the ship," Annette said. "The sooner we can figure out who took Emilio out, the better."

Millie's app chimed. "Time to get back to work. Our Thanksgiving Turkey Trot Parade was so popular, we're rolling out a Candy Cane Christmas Lane Parade. This one will circle around the lido deck instead of going through the atrium. But first, Danielle and I need to head downstairs for an important meeting in the theater."

"Keep me posted," Annette hollered as Danielle and Millie made their way out of the galley.

Millie linked arms with her friend on the way to the stairwell. "Like I said, there's no way you could have killed Emilio. On the flip side, my gut tells me whoever broke into your cabin might come after you."

"You better believe I'll be watching my back."

"And your front and both sides. Don't wander around dark corridors alone at night."

"No kidding. If I end up going overboard, I didn't do it."

Millie abruptly stopped. "I know you're joking. At least, I hope you're joking."

"I am."

Their eyes met, and Millie could see Danielle was becoming emotional. It had been a stressful day, not to mention a long and emotional journey for her friend...carrying around the guilt of her brother's death. Having Emilio contact her out of the blue and dangling the carrot of returning her brother's things, only to have him use her.

Someone was out there, desperate to get their hands on the cocaine, and Danielle was directly in their path, which meant they had to figure out who it was—and fast.

*****

It was back to business by the time Danielle and Millie reached the packed theater with every available elf, snowman, and reindeer on hand. There were dancing Christmas trees, carolers with bright red and white costumes, horn blowing gingerbread men and flute tooting grinches. And it was loud...as in high-volume, high-energy loud.

Millie ran to her office, grabbed Andy's bullhorn, and returned to the stage. "Hellooooo everyone!"

It grew quiet, all eyes turning to their boss. "I feel your excitement and enthusiasm. In fact, I have a challenge. I want this parade to get even more fabulous feedback and five-star ratings from passengers than we did from our Turkey Trot Parade."

Millie glimpsed Andy strolling down the center aisle. "And to help us pull it all together is our expert entertainer, a man we all know and love, Andy Walker."

She stepped off to the side, nearly bursting with pride as rowdy applause ensued. There were catcalls and whistles, stomping feet and loud hoots while her friend and former boss took the stage.

It was the first time Andy had formally met with his former staff since stepping down as the ship's cruise director.

Millie secretly thought he'd put it off because he was still coming to grips with the sudden curveball life had thrown him, not to mention the tight-knit group of entertainment staff was especially close. In other words, Andy was family.

He lifted both hands, the smile never leaving his face. "You know how much I love all of you."

The hooting and hollering picked up again. "We love Andy. We love Andy," they chanted.

Millie joined in, clapping her hands. Andy was getting his official sendoff to his new position, *Siren of the Seas'* entertainment style.

The roar died down again until Andy asked them a question. "How is your new cruise director, Millie, doing?"

A deafening roar filled the theater with more clapping and chanting.

Millie joined Andy on stage, her smile matching his.

"Shall we take a bow?" Andy joked.

"We should, if we want them to stop," Millie shot back.

Linking arms, Andy and Millie took a bow, and then Millie picked up the bullhorn again.

"Andy never got an appropriate sendoff. Many of you have asked me how he's doing, so I figured I would let him tell you himself." Millie tapped his arm.

"Thank you for the cards, the letters, the calls and the prayers. I cherish every single one and am forever grateful for being a part of this team. You made my job easy." Andy paused, and Millie could see he was tearing up, so she quickly jumped in.

"And now he's in charge of fun and funds, which means he'll still be keeping us in line," she joked.

"But will also be right here if Millie needs my help," Andy added. "In fact, she's asked me to help organize the parade, so let's roll up our sleeves and get started."

The next few hours flew by, with Andy and Millie working side by side, organizing, arranging, and planning every step, every detail of the parade. The meeting ended, and the theater cleared.

Millie addressed a few minor issues that popped up. She finished and found Andy seated in the front row, thoughtfully studying her. She offered him a smile and slowly made her way down the side steps.

"Well?" She plopped down in the seat next to him. "How am I doing?"

"Wonderfully. Exactly as I thought you would. You have this, Millie." Andy patted her leg. "Thank you for inviting me. It meant a lot to work with everyone again."

"You're welcome," she said softly. "You know you can stop by anytime."

"I appreciate it. I may take you up on the offer."

"The door, or should I say the stage curtains, will always be open."

"How was your day?" Andy turned to face her. "I heard you and your friends took an excursion and it didn't end well."

"You have no idea." Millie started to fill him in when she heard a loud *thud* echoing from somewhere behind the curtain. A bloodcurdling scream followed.

Chapter 22

Millie sprang from the theater chair. "What was that?"

"I don't know, but it came from somewhere near the back of the stage." Andy pointed toward the curtains. "Someone is back there."

Millie, with Andy hot on her heels, ran to the side steps, bolted to the top and hurried to the prop storage area where they found Mervin flat on his back. Flash, the dummy, was sprawled out next to him.

"Ahh." Mervin let out a low moan.

Millie dropped to her knees. "What happened?"

"Mervin tripped over a stupid reindeer prop," Flash explained.

Sure enough, a red-nosed reindeer, his left front leg bent at an odd angle, was shoved up against a portable North Pole light.

"It was dark. Mervin couldn't see where he was going and tripped," Flash said. "I think we need to get checked out."

"What were you two doing, creeping around back here in the dark?" Andy asked.

"Ahh." Mervin moaned loudly.

"I'll call medical." Millie stepped to the side and requested a wheelchair or stretcher and someone to transport the ventriloquist to the medical center.

A small army of security guards, medical staff, and the requested items arrived within minutes.

The ship's head nurse, Gavin Framm, was with them and quickly assessed the situation. With the help of two other members of the ship's safety team, they got Mervin, who refused to part with Flash, into the wheelchair.

The safety team members carefully wheeled Mervin and Flash down the side ramp, up the center aisle, and out of the theater.

Gavin Framm stayed behind. "What's up with the dummy doing all the talking?"

"You got me," Millie shrugged. "For some reason, Flash does most of the talking. What do you think?"

Gavin tipped his hand back and forth. "I'm sure Doctor Gundervan will order some x-rays. Between the three of us, I don't think he's seriously injured, although I could be wrong."

Millie's heart plummeted. "That's what I thought. The guy is a pain in the Rumpelstiltskin."

"The good news is that he's only on board for a few short weeks," Andy said.

"A few short weeks too many," Millie groaned. "I smell a potential lawsuit."

"Unfortunately, I was getting the same impression," her former boss said grimly.

Gavin made a move to leave. "I'm heading back to the medical center now and will explain what happened to Doctor Gundervan."

"I'll call down and check on him shortly," Millie promised. "But first, I need to fill Nic and Donovan Sweeney in."

"Would you like me to go with you?" Andy asked after Gavin left.

"No. I appreciate the offer. This shouldn't take long."

On her way up to the bridge, Millie radioed Donovan and asked him to meet her there.

She arrived to find the ship preparing for departure, which meant the bridge was full.

Nic caught his wife's eye and made his way over. "You're not downstairs verifying all passengers and crewmembers are back on board?"

"No. Andy and I were busy ironing out some of the parade details. I was getting ready to head down to the gangway when Mervin, the ventriloquist, tripped over a reindeer. I called medical. They showed up and took him to be checked out."

"He's injured?"

"Maybe. Maybe not." Millie told him she'd radioed for Donovan to join them. "I didn't realize you would be right in the middle of departure. We can hold off on this until a little later."

"We might have to."

Millie called Donovan, postponing the meeting for another hour, and then headed home. She found her pup standing in front of the sliders, gazing out with a longing look on his face.

"Let's get some fresh air." Millie stepped onto the balcony, her eyes drawn to the vendors who were packing up for the day. From her vantage point, she could clearly see how it would have been possible for Emilio to set up shop, both legal and illegal, from the spot.

All he needed was a few solid partners—crewmembers from the various ships that docked there, maybe even cargo ship crewmembers.

The big mystery, at least to Millie, was why Emilio had used Danielle to transport the drugs to St. Kitts. Surely he knew about her background in law enforcement. But then, perhaps he thought she would be the perfect cover.

Had Emilio double-crossed his original partner, an employee of *Siren of the Seas*?

Millie played catch with Scout and let him splash in his pool while she watched their ship drift away from the dock. She leaned over the railing, gazing toward the outboard wing and spotted one of the staff captains, binoculars in hand, as they navigated their way out into open water.

The harbor pilot's boat skimmed past, which meant it was safe for Millie to track Donovan down and meet with Nic. She coaxed Scout back inside and heard a knock on the door.

The ship's purser stood on the other side. "I was getting ready to call you to see if you had time to meet," Millie said.

"I just left the infirmary," Donovan said. "It appears Mervin, at least according to what his dummy, Flash, told me, won't be returning to the stage anytime soon."

Chapter 23

"Mervin is planning to sue us," Millie guessed.

"It's possible. If Mervin, instead of that dummy, had talked, I might have gotten a better feel for the situation. When he did talk, the two repeated what the other said. It was very distracting." Donovan tapped the side of his forehead. "I think the man might be missing a few marbles, if you know what I mean."

"You could be right." Millie rubbed her brow. "Have you talked to Nic about it yet?"

"No. I figured since you were in the vicinity when it happened, not to mention it was in your department, you should be there." Donovan held the door while Millie grabbed her lanyard and stepped out into the hall.

The bridge had cleared, leaving only key personnel in place and giving Nic, Donovan and

Millie privacy to discuss their latest crisis—Mervin the ventriloquist.

"How was he hurt?" Nic slipped his reading glasses on, studying Doctor Gundervan's official report. "It says here he strained a muscle."

"He tripped over a reindeer. Andy and I found him sprawled out on the floor with his dummy next to him," Millie said.

"Maybe the dummy tripped him," Nic joked.

Millie shivered involuntarily. "Could be. The thing is creepy as all get out."

"It does most of the talking," Donovan said.

Nic arched a brow. "The dummy?"

"Mervin, the ventriloquist, rarely talks. When he does, the two repeat what the other said."

"That's odd," Nic said.

"You're telling me. Gundervan and I spoke privately. He thinks Mervin is experiencing some pain, but not to the degree he's claiming."

"Wonderful," Nic said sarcastically. "Just what we need. A slip and fall entertainer."

"He signed the standard agreement, waiving his right to sue," Millie said.

"Which has never stopped anyone before." Donovan flipped his file folder open and slid a piece of paper across the table. "This is his current list of demands."

Nic picked it up. "Access to a motorized scooter, cane and wheelchair. Transfer to a cabin with wheelchair accessible facilities. In-room assistance for Flash and Mervin."

"What does he mean by in-room assistance?" Millie interrupted.

"He wants someone on call twenty-four seven," Donovan said. "He also mentioned contacting an attorney about safety on board the ship."

"And you said the only thing he has is a pulled muscle?"

"Correct."

Nic set the paper aside, leaned back in his chair, and closed his eyes. "Where do we find these people?"

"It wasn't me," Millie said. "He was scheduled before I took over. Not that I'm trying to throw Andy under the bus, but I have enough of my own issues to deal with."

"Because of Danielle, the body you found along the side of the road and the suitcase with cocaine," Nic said.

"Body?"

"It's a long story." Millie could feel the heat of Donovan's intense gaze. "Patterson set up a sting to catch the guy who hid the cocaine in Danielle's suitcase. It backfired. We found the guy's body on the side of the road leading to Brimstone Hill while our tour guide was changing a flat tire."

"Patterson believes the cause of death was blunt force trauma," Nic said.

"Desmond, our tour guide, remembers Emilio. He had a vendor stand down by the port. I think he was using it as a front." Millie briefly laid out her theory. "I think Emilio partnered with crewmembers on board ships, including *Siren of the Seas*. For some reason, he tried getting the cocaine to St. Kitts using Danielle. Emilio's connection found out and attempted to grab the suitcase before Danielle. Whoever it was, was in the cargo storage area, conked her on the head, but before he/she/they could grab the goods and get away, Sharky showed up."

Donovan picked up. "Which is why someone broke into Danielle's cabin and ransacked the lost and found."

"And they're still looking for the suitcase and cocaine," Millie said. "I'm sure they realize by now that Patterson has it in a secure location, so it looks like a potential killer and drug dealer is going to get away. Or maybe not. Maybe they're so desperate the person or persons will keep looking for it."

Nic grimaced. "I don't like the sounds of this at all."

"Me either. There is one glimmer of hope...Desmond, our tour guide and driver. We all chipped in and gave him some cash to help figure out what Emilio was up to and who his contacts may have been."

"Because he works at the port where Emilio was fronting his shop," Nic guessed.

"And he remembers Emilio. Not to mention Desmond has a slight crush on Danielle, and I think he legitimately wants to help. There's one more thing." Millie shoved her chair back. "We might have a solid clue about the crewmember on board. I'll be right back."

She ran to the apartment, grabbed the printouts, the still frames of the lost and found "ransacker" along with the image of the person breaking into Danielle's cabin and returned to the table. "Emilio sold St. Kitts & Nevis Patriots' sports memorabilia. The reflective logo on this person's jacket matches the logo, which means we can link this person to Emilio."

"That's a longshot, Millie," Nic said.

"Maybe not if Desmond can confirm what Emilio was actually peddling at the port."

Donovan's cell phone chimed. "I'm late for another meeting. What would you like to do about Mervin's list of demands?"

"Do we have a wheelchair-accessible cabin available?" Nic asked.

"We do."

"Move him in there. Let him have the scooter, if we have any left, the cane, the wheelchair and time off."

"And someone to assist him?" Donovan asked.

"He can have room service delivery, that's it. I'm not catering to someone who has a pulled muscle."

"I agree." Donovan headed out while Millie began gathering up her papers. "Desmond planned to jump on it pretty quickly, which means we might have additional information in a day or so."

"Reading between the lines, I wouldn't plan on Flash and Mervin returning to work anytime soon," Nic said.

"Which might be a blessing in disguise. I don't mean to sound callous, but the guy wasn't cutting it. He insulted passengers and the dummy doing the talking is disturbing." Millie dropped the clues off at home and ran upstairs to track down Tara Daughtery, a ship's dancer, for *Limbo on the Lido*.

The rest of her afternoon passed by in a blur. The highlight of the evening was hosting the high-energy musical and theatrical performance, *Gem of the Sea*.

Millie stood on the sidelines, humming along while the singers and dancers performed on stage. With two costume changes, the piles of clothing and accessories grew, and she began sorting and putting things away.

Danielle arrived during intermission and offered to help. "I heard about Mervin's fall. How's he doing?" she asked as she handed Millie a feathered boa.

"I don't know." Millie marked the checklist and reached for an empty hanger. "He pulled a muscle and has been hinting at hiring a lawyer. Nic and Donovan agreed to move him to a wheelchair-accessible cabin, give him unlimited access to room service, a scooter, and some other equipment to help him get around."

"The guy is a nutjob," Danielle said. "Have you tried talking to him? I mean, to his dummy?"

"Not recently. I kind of hope he decides to go home."

"You and me both."

The final strains of the last number echoed, and Millie hustled back to the stage to wrap things up. The entertainment staff crowded into the dressing room, and there was a buzz of excitement and energy in the air, the magic that always occurred after the headliner shows.

Kevin, one of the head dancers, sashayed across the floor. He wiggled out of a pair of Elton John silver glitter platform shoes and slid them onto the shelf. "I love our Gem of the Sea show. I hope it never ends. Did you happen to notice we got a standing ovation?"

"I did." Millie grinned. "And you deserved it. The show was fabulous. I'm so proud of all of you."

"I heard Mervin took a tumble. How are he and his freakish sidekick, Flash?"

"Resting comfortably in a wheelchair-accessible cabin with unlimited access to a scooter and room service."

"He's faking it," Kevin said.

"How do you know?"

"Because I saw him going into one of the bathroom stalls across from the crew dining room about an hour ago. He was getting around with no issues."

Millie's eyes narrowed. "You're kidding."

"Nope."

"That is so wrong." Danielle slid the feathered headpiece on the shelf. "How are we going to prove it?"

"What's most important to Mervin?"

"Flash," Kevin said. "Those two are joined at the hip."

"Let me give it some thought," Millie said. "I'll figure out a way to expose Mervin and Flash if it's the last thing I do."

Chapter 24

Millie bolted upright in bed, the alarm clock blaring loudly. "Ugh," she groaned, rolling over to shut it off. "What time is it?"

"Early. It's early and another port day."

"What island are we visiting? Bermuda?"

Nic chuckled. "Close, if we were over a thousand miles to the north. We're stopping in Antigua."

"Antigua. I knew that." Millie pressed a hand to her forehead. "These islands are all running together. All of them except St. Kitts. I'll never forget Brimstone Hill, the treacherous trek to Romney Manor, and I know Cat will never forget the monkeys."

"Monkeys?"

"It's a long story. One of them stole her sunglasses."

"I can't wait to hear it. Maybe you can tell me about it during our date day later today. We both have a couple of hours off this afternoon." Nic flung the covers back and swung his legs over the side of the bed.

"I like the sounds of having a couple of hours off." Millie nudged their pup away from the headboard. "You get ready first. Scout and I will run downstairs and start a pot of coffee."

By the time Nic joined her, the coffee was ready, and she'd whipped up a plate of scrambled eggs, made toast, and even microwaved slices of bacon.

She fed Scout and followed Nic onto the balcony to watch the sun come up. "It's going to be a beautiful day in Bermuda."

"Antigua," Nic corrected.

"I know. I was kidding." Millie handed him a plate, placed hers on the small table, and gave Scout a small piece of egg. "I'm going to visit

Mervin and Flash today. I think he's faking and I plan on proving it."

"How?"

"I don't know. I haven't figured that part out yet. Patterson is also on my to-do list. I'm worried about Danielle's safety."

"For good reason, although if someone on board the ship is after the suitcase, they must realize it's locked up and in a secure location."

"You would think so."

The couple joined hands and prayed for a safe port day for the crew and passengers. They also prayed Emilio's killer would be caught and if Mervin was faking his injury, the truth would come out.

"What's on the agenda for date day?" Millie scooped a heaping spoonful of eggs on top of her toast, added a slice of bacon, and stuck her other piece of toast on top.

"Acupuncture. I figured we could both use a session."

Millie, who had taken a big bite, began choking on her food. "Acupuncture? No way. Been there, done that."

"I'm kidding," Nic laughed. "Seriously, it's something we'll both enjoy and benefit from."

Despite her pleading, flirting, and begging, Nic refused to tell her what he had planned.

His radio went off. It was Captain Vitale summoning him to the bridge to greet the harbor pilot, who was getting ready to board.

"Gotta run." Nic reached for his empty plate and Millie stopped him. "I'll take care of this."

She made quick work of putting the kitchen back in order. Millie showered and dressed, arriving right on time for her early morning staff meeting, and then headed to the gangway with Danielle to see the first passengers off the ship.

"Are you gonna do the Andy speech?" Danielle nudged her. "You missed it yesterday."

Millie wrinkled her nose. "I dunno."

"C'mon. It's cute. Besides, the passengers love it."

"I..."

"You at least need to say something, even if it's just wishing everyone a good day and reminding them not to forget the sunscreen."

"I suppose you're right." Millie trudged over to the phone box, lifted the receiver, and punched in the numbers to access the intercom system.

"Well...good morning, ladies and gentlemen. This is your cruise die wreck tore, Millie Armati. Let me be the first to welcome you to the beautiful island of Antigua. Today's forecast is warm and sunny with only a chance of thunderstorms late this afternoon. Don't forget to stay on the ship's time and don't forget the sunscreen. Whatever your plans, I hope you have a wonderful day." She hung the receiver up and returned to Danielle's side.

"See? That wasn't so bad."

"I think my voice sounds whiny. Good morning ladies and gentlemen," she mocked in a deep voice.

Danielle chuckled. "You don't sound like that."

A group of passengers stopped by, asking questions about the port area and the back on board deadline. Millie waited until they were alone again. "Are you going to call Desmond to see if he found anything out about Emilio?"

"Yeah. I figured I would wait until around eight-thirty. His tours start at nine, so I thought I could try to catch him before he got busy."

The crowds thinned, the tour groups departed, and Nic appeared.

"Hello, Captain Armati," Danielle greeted him. "Millie mentioned you have a few hours off this afternoon."

"We do. I've planned a special surprise," he said. "And how are you doing, young lady? Have you had anyone else break down your cabin door?"

"Nope. I'm sure Millie mentioned our St. Kitts tour guide is trying to get a little intel on Emilio."

"She did. I hope between him and Dave Patterson, we're able to figure out who might be behind it."

"You and me both." Danielle excused herself and Nic waited until she was gone. "Doctor Gundervan called a few minutes ago. He wants to chat about Mervin Goldsmith."

"Uh-oh. Did he say why?"

Nic shook his head. "I thought you should be there, considering the circumstances."

The couple grew quiet as they made their way to the medical center, only steps away from the gangway.

The woman behind the desk summoned the doctor, who arrived promptly and escorted them to his office in the back. "I visited Mr. Goldsmith in his cabin a short time ago."

"How is he?" Nic asked.

"He's complaining of back pain, leg pain and now he seems to think he's having issues with his memory." The doctor leaned forward in his chair. "I'm quite confident his symptoms are being exaggerated."

"Meaning you think he's faking it," Nic said.

"Precisely. His x-rays back up my diagnosis. I found no swelling, no signs of bruising. He mentioned an attorney again. I think he's trying to set us up for a lawsuit. In fact, he asked me to prescribe..." The doctor reached for his pad of paper. "Psilocybin for what he claims is the onset of depression."

"Psilocybin," Millie repeated. "What is that?"

"A hallucinogenic drug recently approved for use in certain US states, while still illegal in others."

Millie blinked rapidly. "Mervin is on drugs?"

"No wonder he lets his dummy do all the talking." Nic's jaw tightened. "So now what?"

"I told him I'm not allowed to sell psilocybin. Instead, I prescribed a very mild antidepressant similar to Prozac."

Millie's mind whirled. Mervin on drugs, recently joining *Siren of the Seas*. What if *he* was the one behind Danielle's attack? She quickly dismissed the idea. Unlike the ship's crewmembers, he didn't have access to the port. "I think he's faking it too. He was barely hurt. In fact, the reindeer sustained greater injury than he and his dummy, and I'm going to prove it."

The couple exited the doctor's office. They reached the bank of elevators when Millie heard someone calling her name.

She turned to find Danielle coming up behind them, waving her cell phone in the air. "Desmond left a message. He said he has information on Emilio that I'm going to want to hear."

"Great." Millie rubbed her hands together. "Let's call him back."

"First, we get Patterson involved." Nic reached for his radio. "Dave Patterson, do you copy?"

"Go ahead Captain Armati."

"I need to meet you in your office as soon as possible."

"I'm on my way."

The trio backtracked, quickly making their way to the security office.

Patterson, with Oscar by his side, arrived at almost the same time. "What happened? Don't tell me Millie's in trouble again."

"Again?" Millie frowned. "When's the last time I was in trouble?"

Patterson started to say something, and Millie stopped him. "Don't answer that."

"Good, because we would be here all day if I had to list them all."

Danielle snickered.

"You're right up there with her."

Her smile vanished. "It's almost always been for a good cause."

"Key word being almost." Patterson unlocked his office door and led them inside. "What do we have?"

"Desmond, our contact in St. Kitts left a message for me. He said he had something on Emilio."

"Let's get to it."

Danielle turned her cell phone on and tapped the screen.

"Hello, Miss Danielle." Desmond's booming voice filled the room. "How are you today?"

"Okay. I'm hoping even better after hearing what you found. Just to let you know, I have you on speaker. I'm with Millie, Siren of the Seas' head of security, and the ship's captain."

"I see. Hello."

"Good morning," Patterson replied. "Danielle said you might have some information about Emilio Torres."

"I don't know what happened to him, but I do know he was involved in a very dangerous business which could easily have caused his death."

Chapter 25

Desmond paused for a second, allowing his statement to sink in. "Have you ever heard the name Jiggy?"

"No," Patterson and Nic said in unison.

"Jiggy, Jermaine Bilmow, is our island's underground pharmaceutical representative."

"Pharmaceutical representative," Patterson repeated. "You mean drug dealer?"

"Major drug dealer. He was seen talking with Mr. Torres shortly before we found his body in the bushes yesterday morning."

Millie could feel the blood drain from her face. A major player drug dealer. Not a small potatoes guy from Chicago, but a drug kingpin. "What about the vendor business down by the port? You said you thought you saw Emilio selling sportswear and memorabilia."

"He was. I showed his picture around to the other vendors. He had a small tent selling St. Kitts & Nevis Patriots merchandise."

"The logo of a man wearing a spiked green helmet," Millie said.

"Correct."

Patterson spoke. "Are you hearing what may have caused Emilio's death? Was it a drug deal fallout?"

"Mr. Torres was stepping on Jiggy's toes, trying to move in on his territory," Desmond said. "I discovered one more thing about the dead man you will find most interesting. He was making friends with many of the visiting cruise ships' crewmembers."

"Making friends?" Millie asked.

"Giving them free stuff."

Millie nearly fell out of her chair. "Free stuff as in Patriots' goods in exchange for…"

"You tell me," Desmond said.

"To make connections and friends, to help him move drugs from the US to St. Kitts," Danielle whispered in a low voice.

"I appreciate the money and I know I offered my help, but I don't want to be on Jiggy's radar, if you know what I mean," Desmond said. "Asking too many questions will put a target on my back."

"We understand," Patterson replied. "You've been a huge help."

"I have done this for Miss Danielle. She is a nice lady and I would hate to see something bad happen to her."

Millie nudged Danielle and pointed to the phone.

"Yes…uh. Next time we visit St. Kitts, I owe you lunch."

Millie could almost see Desmond smiling through the phone, and his voice softened. "I would like that very much."

"Thank you, Desmond," Danielle said sincerely. "You have no idea how much you helped."

"You are welcome. We will talk soon."

The call ended, and Danielle waved her phone in the air. "That's it. Emilio befriended crewmembers from the various ships who stopped at the port, gave them stuff and then convinced them to help him move drugs."

"I bet he gave them more than sports memorabilia. Someone on board our ship, a crewmember, has a Patriots jacket," Millie said. "If we can find the jacket and owner, we'll have Emilio's contact and possibly his killer."

She sprang from her chair and started to pace. "There are only a certain number of crewmembers who would have been able to leave the ship early yesterday morning."

"Correct," Patterson agreed.

"It had to have been someone who worked near or on the dock with access to transporting goods."

"Two for two," Nic said.

"Sharky knows who they are." Patterson pressed his palms together. "I'll have Sharky supply me with a list and schedule a meeting with them."

Danielle picked up. "During the meeting, you could have someone else search their cabins for the jacket."

"Finding the jacket won't prove anything," Nic said. "Even if you find it, it doesn't prove the crewmember was part of a drug trafficking ring. They could have purchased the jacket as a souvenir."

"True," Patterson agreed. "Unless we can find traces of drugs and we have someone very special on board who can."

"Fin." Millie snapped her fingers. "That's brilliant. Fin can sniff out the drugs."

"Brilliant?" Nic grinned. "You're sounding more and more like Andy every day."

"It will take a little time to get the list and set up the meeting," Patterson warned.

"I would like to tag along, if you don't mind," Millie said.

"Me too," Danielle chimed in. "Besides, we can speed up the process."

"Because you two are old pros at searching cabins."

"We won't contaminate potential evidence." Millie made a cross on her chest. "Promise."

"I dunno." Patterson shot Nic a look. "What do you think, boss?"

"It's up to you. Even if you say no, I have a feeling my wife will find a way to insert herself into the investigation."

"You're right." Patterson heaved a heavy sigh. "I suppose it would be better to just invite you two to come along than to have you blow in, magnifying glasses blazing."

"Sweet." Danielle clapped her hands. "Finally, an investigation you've officially invited us to be a part of."

"I never thought I would see the day." Millie gave Danielle a high five. "It's probably a good thing setting it up will take a little time because I have another small project I need to work on. It's called the Mervin and Flash Con Game."

Chapter 26

The rest of Millie's morning passed uneventfully. She hosted a round of trivia, "All about Antigua," followed by bingo. She popped in during a past guest luncheon and munched on finger sandwiches, feasted on her favorite French onion soup, washing it all down with a serving of fresh fruit and cream for dessert.

It wasn't until the luncheon ended that Millie had time to track down her friend, Nikki Tan, who worked at guest services.

"Hello, Millie," Nikki greeted her with a smile. "How are you?"

"Busy. Running nonstop."

Nikki pointed her finger up. "Your announcements sound very professional, just like Andy's."

"Thanks. I think I'm finally getting my groove." Millie changed the subject. "I'm hoping you can help me."

"I'll try."

"I need to find out what cabin Donovan put Mervin Goldsmith, the ventriloquist, in."

"The entertainer who was injured and needed a wheelchair-accessible cabin?"

"Yes."

"Let me check." Nikki tapped the keyboard. "He's in A4420."

"One of the lower deck balcony cabins."

"Correct." Nikki's brows furrowed.

"What is it?"

"The passengers in A4422 complained about loud noises coming from Mervin's cabin this morning."

"Loud noises?"

"The caller described it as thunking, clunking and chanting."

"Chanting," Millie repeated. "So, Mervin and Flash are moving around inside making weird noises."

"According to this passenger's complaint."

"I need to find out what that man is up to."

"He is very odd," Nikki said. "He was down here earlier, demanding a different scooter, except he wasn't the one doing the talking."

"His dummy was."

"Yep."

"You said a passenger in A4422 lodged a complaint. What about the cabin on the other side of Mervin? Is that one empty?"

"Nope." Nikki shook her head. "Both cabins are occupied."

Millie absentmindedly gazed out the window at a small sailboat skimming across the tranquil turquoise water. "There has to be a way to figure out what he's doing."

"The passenger in 4422 also asked to be moved."

"Moved?" Millie's eyes lit. "As in, moved to another cabin and vacating the one next to Mervin?"

"Correct. I told him I would need to clear it with a supervisor."

"That's it." Millie clapped her hands. "Move the guest to another cabin and I can set up surveillance inside 4422."

Nikki studied the screen. "We have a same class empty cabin available. Actually, it's in a better location. Unfortunately, Donovan is a hard sell on moving passengers."

Millie's eyes slid toward Donovan's office, located directly behind guest services. "Is he in his office?"

"Yeah. At least, I think so."

"I'll be right back."

Millie circled behind the passengers waiting in line and approached the door behind guest services. She gave it a light rap and heard a muffled reply.

Easing the door open, she stuck her head around the corner.

"Good morning, Millie."

"Morning, Donovan. Do you have a minute?"

"For you I have two." Donovan motioned her inside. "What's up?"

"I'm sure you remember Mervin, the ventriloquist, who tripped over the reindeer yesterday and is claiming he's injured."

"How can I forget? I spoke to Doctor Gundervan a few minutes ago. He said Mervin is asking for some potent drugs and he thinks he's not as injured as he's leading us to believe. I've asked our safety crew to inspect the backstage area to make sure it doesn't happen again."

"I take full responsibility for the entertainment staff, equipment and safety of the people who work under me." Millie eased into the chair opposite him. "He's faking it. The reindeer sustained more injuries than Mervin and his dummy."

"I suspect you're right, but how do we prove it?"

"I'm glad you asked. Nikki told me the passenger in the cabin next to Mervin complained he's making noise and banging around."

"Banging around?" Donovan made an unhappy sound. "Maybe he's practicing driving the scooter and is banging it into the wall."

"While listening to meditation and chanting music? I doubt it. I'm here to ask you to move the passengers in A4422 so I can set up surveillance in their cabin."

"Set up surveillance?"

"To find out what he's up to." Millie could see Donovan was considering her request, and hurried on. "If he's faking it and plans to hire a lawyer, it will cost a lot more than the inconvenience of moving the passenger to another cabin."

"Do we have an empty cabin available?"

"Yeah. They already asked to be moved. Give them an upgrade to a better deck and I guarantee they'll jump all over it."

"I don't know."

"Please? I feel somewhat responsible for the incident and this would be my way of resolving the issue."

"True. I suppose it wouldn't hurt." Donovan wagged his finger at her. "Don't do anything against company policy. It could backfire on you."

"You mean like sneaking into his cabin?"

"Precisely."

"I'll do my best," Millie promised. "No guarantees on that one, but one thing I can guarantee, if Mervin is faking it, I'm going to find out."

*****

After Millie told Nikki to contact the passenger and offer to move them to an upgraded cabin and to let her know when the move was done, she headed to the galley. It was time to set up a surveillance schedule.

Annette was wrapping up the last few lunch orders. Millie waited until she caught her eye and joined her.

"You look like a monkey just stole your sunglasses," Annette joked.

Millie grinned. "I'll never forget the look on Cat's face."

"It was priceless."

"I need help."

"Tracking down Danielle's attacker?"

"No, although that's in the works." Millie briefly filled her friend in on the phone call from Desmond.

Annette let out a low whistle. "Wow. I have faith in Fin. If there's even a trace of drugs in those crewmembers' cabins, Fin will find it."

"I agree," Millie said. "My more pressing issue is Mervin Goldsmith."

"The oddball ventriloquist."

"Yep. He tripped over a reindeer backstage, ended up in medical, is claiming a serious injury and hinting at hiring an attorney."

"Do you think it's possible he has a legit injury?"

Millie made a thumbs down. "I don't think he's as bad off as he's letting on. Doctor Gundervan doesn't either, and I intend to prove it."

"How?"

"By spying on him. Donovan moved him to a passenger cabin. According to Nikki, who works in guest services, his neighbor is complaining about weird noises and lots of thumping and bumping."

"Could be he's trying to get used to using the scooter or wheelchair."

"While listening to chanting music? I think he's doing something else."

"You have a plan."

"Donovan agreed to move the complaining passenger to an upgraded balcony cabin. As soon as they're gone, I'm setting up surveillance in the empty cabin. This is where the needing help part comes in."

"To monitor his movements," Annette guessed. "Patterson won't let you sneak in there or put a camera inside to spy on him."

"Nope, but he can't stop us from monitoring activity from the balcony," Millie said. "I was thinking we could work in shifts. You, me, Cat, maybe even Danielle."

Amit, who had been quietly listening, spoke. "I would like to help."

"Lunch is over," Annette said. "I can take the first shift and Amit can cover the second."

"I can handle the third. If need be, I'll call Cat later to see if she can help, since the gift shop is closed until this evening." With a plan in place and Annette on standby, waiting for word that the cabin was clear, Millie hustled to the library for her craft class.

Nikki's call came midway through the class. Millie excused herself, promising to return shortly, and texted Annette, who met her outside the empty cabin. The women slipped inside and immediately heard rhythmic sounds.

...ting...ting...ting...tong...tong...tong.

"What in the world?" Annette frowned.

"It sounds like those singing bowls."

"Singing bowls?"

"I watched a show about it one time. It's for deep meditation."

"Did you try it?"

"No. Praying works way better."

"You said it." Annette slid the balcony slider open, grabbed the desk chair and settled in. "Might as well make myself comfy."

"Do you have your phone to record potential evidence?" Millie asked.

Annette patted her pocket. "Right here. Amit will take over in an hour and a half, just in time for me to start meal prep."

"And I can handle the next shift. Thanks, Annette."

"You're welcome. I hope we catch him."

"Me too." Millie returned to the craft class, keeping her cell phone close by, waiting for Annette's call.

The class ended. Up next was a Q&A with the cruise director, something Millie had added after discovering how many passengers were interested in what went on "behind-the-scenes."

Danielle joined her, and despite being a port day, the lounge was packed. The women fielded questions ranging from the size of the crewmembers' cabins to their favorite activities.

The Q&A ran over. Millie answered a few more questions. She began escorting the last two passengers to the door when her cell phone chimed. It was a text from Amit. *You need to get up here.*

Chapter 27

Millie texted Amit back. *On my way.* She took the side stairs two at a time, racing down to the Atlantic deck. She jogged around the corner and found Amit standing in the doorway, waiting for her.

As Millie drew closer, she could hear the *tong, tong,* noises coming from Mervin's cabin. She stepped inside and found they were even louder, loud enough to shake the wall. "How long has this been going on?"

"Since I texted you. I do not know what that man is doing over there." Amit told her he'd ordered room service, a cart full of food. "He came into the hallway wearing a neck brace, took the food, but did not tip the delivery person."

"Cheapskate," Millie muttered.

"It was quiet for five, maybe ten minutes and then I started hearing these noises."

"This is ridiculous. I'm sure he's annoying the passengers on the other side."

"I would think so. There is also this." Amit held a finger to his lips and led Millie to the balcony slider.

She tiptoed outside and could hear the chanting music, not as loud but still audible, and caught a movement on the other side of the privacy panel. Easing onto her hands and knees, she lowered her head and gazed through the narrow gap between the panel and deck. A pair of crossed legs were clearly visible.

Mervin was doing yoga on the balcony. Easing her cell phone from her pocket, she tapped the screen and snapped a picture before returning inside and quietly sliding the door shut.

"He's doing yoga," she hissed.

"Yes. That is what I thought."

"I knew it. I knew he was faking."

"You have proof now," Amit said.

"Yes, but not enough."

"Slip your phone around the corner and snap a picture."

"Too risky. I need to smoke him out."

Amit's eyes widened in horror. "Miss Millie. Starting any sort of fire on board a ship is very dangerous. You remember what happened with the cordon bleu."

"It's a figure of speech. It means to drive him out of hiding." Millie snapped her fingers. "That's it. Carmine."

"Carmine?"

"The head of engineering. I need to find out if there's a way to make an emergency announcement to Mervin's cabin and then cut the power."

"Scare him into blowing his cover," Amit said. "You are very clever."

"Not yet. Don't start heaping on the Millie-you're-so-awesome praise until we figure out if it will work."

Carmine wasn't someone Millie phoned regularly, so it took her a few tries to track him down.

"Hello, Millie Armati," Carmine greeted her. "Congratulations on your recent promotion. I love hearing your lovely voice every day."

"Thank you, Carmine. I think I'm finally finding my groove. I have a quick question for you. Is it possible to make an announcement and also cut the power to only one cabin?"

"It is possible."

"The reason I'm asking is I want to flush someone out of their cabin, making it appear to be an emergency."

"Someone is refusing to leave their cabin?" Carmine asked. "Perhaps this is something security should handle."

Millie was on the fence about how much she should share, but decided she needed help and was willing to risk it. "I believe someone in my department is faking an injury and thought if we could kill the power to the cabin and make it seem like there's an emergency, I could find out pretty darn quick how injured they are."

There was silence on the other end of the line, lasting so long Millie thought she and Carmine had been disconnected. "Hello?"

"I'm still here. I was thinking about if this might get me in trouble."

"The potential is always there, but I can assure you I'll take one hundred percent responsibility."

"I…"

"Please? I'll owe you one." Millie figured it was time to try a Sharky-style bribe. "I'll have a specially prepared meal delivered right to your door."

"A gourmet dinner?" Carmine perked up. "What kind?"

"Whatever you want."

"I love steak and lobster."

"Steak and lobster it is. What would you like to go along with it?"

"Would a loaded baked potato, tossed salad, and baked asparagus be too much trouble?"

Millie repeated the order. "You would like surf and turf, a loaded baked potato, baked asparagus and a tossed salad. What kind of dressing?"

"French."

"French," Millie said. "Amit, who works alongside Annette in the galley, is standing next to me and has your order. When and where would you like it delivered?"

"To the engineering office at six. Seven if six is too early."

Millie shifted the phone. "Six or seven delivered to the engineering office, Amit?"

"Six will be fine," Amit said.

"You have yourself a deal," Millie replied. "About the announcement and cutting the power."

"I'll have to be on hand to supervise. It would only be for a short amount of time?"

"Maybe a minute or two." Millie gave him their cabin number and asked him to keep it on the down low.

She ended the call and triumphantly waved her cell phone in the air. "Carmine is on his way."

*****

As promised, the chief engineer arrived moments later. "What if this backfires and the guy is genuinely injured?"

"Then I take full responsibility for what happens," Millie said.

"I dunno."

"Do not forget about the steak and lobster," Amit reminded him. "I will make sure you get the choicest piece of meat. It will melt in your mouth."

Carmine smacked his lips. "I can already taste it."

"And the gourmet meal is all yours for only a couple minutes of your time." Millie motioned to Amit. "Take a quick peek outside and make sure Mervin is still in his cabin."

Amit ran out, returning within seconds. "He is no longer on the balcony. The curtains are open and I can see someone moving around inside."

"Perfect." Millie turned to Carmine. "As soon as I make the announcement to abandon ship, cut the power."

"And I will start banging on the wall," Amit said. "I hope this works."

"It will. Mervin is all about Mervin and Flash. He's going to run for his life."

Using the laptop he brought with him, Carmine accessed the shipboard system, pressed several keys and entered multiple passwords. "I'm ready for you to make the announcement."

Millie hesitated, envisioning something going wrong and mistakenly making an "abandon ship" announcement ship wide. "You're positive the only person who will hear the announcement is in the cabin next door."

"A thousand percent," Carmine said. "Remember, my neck is on the line too."

"Right. And the power...only the power next door."

"Correct."

"Here we go."

"Give me the signal, Millie." Amit stood next to the wall between them and Mervin.

"Go."

Amit began pounding loudly on the wall and screaming.

Millie cleared her throat and pressed the announcement button. "All passengers and crew. Ladies and gentlemen. There's been an emergency.

Please immediately proceed to your muster station for further instructions. I repeat...please immediately proceed to your muster station."

Amit continued pounding. Carmine tapped the keys. "The power is out."

Millie ran into the hall and began pounding on Mervin's door. "Abandon ship! Abandon ship!"

The cabin door flew open. A wild-eyed Mervin wearing a robe and clutching Flash ran out of the cabin, dragging a carry-on suitcase behind him. He sprinted down the hallway while Millie videotaped it with her cell phone.

"Well?" Amit stepped in next to her. "Did you get it?"

"Every second of Mervin abandoning ship." Millie grinned. "It appears he's made a miraculous recovery."

Chapter 28

Nic was already waiting in the apartment when Millie arrived for their "date day" afternoon. He met her at the door and presented her with a single red rose. "For my beautiful wife."

"For me?" Millie's heart fluttered as Nic placed a light kiss on her lips. "I've missed you."

"I've missed you too. With my recent promotion, I feel like we're two ships passing in the night."

"Passing in the day, passing in the night," Nic joked. "It doesn't help we've had several crises. Danielle's attack, Mervin's slip and fall."

"I don't think Mervin is going to be a problem for much longer." Millie's expression grew mischievous as she turned her cell phone on and played the video of Mervin and Flash running down the hall.

"How did you get this?"

"I tricked him into thinking the ship was in trouble and he needed to vacate his cabin immediately."

"Tricked him? It must have been a pretty slick trick."

"I needed a little help. Coercing with food is such an easy way. I…"

Nic placed a light finger against her lips. "I'm not sure I want the details."

Millie laughed. "No. You probably don't. Let's just say Patterson has a copy. He, along with Donovan and Doctor Gundervan, met with Mervin. He wasn't happy about being tricked, but I say it all worked out in the end."

"And Danielle. Is Patterson still working on figuring out who attacked her and broke into her cabin?"

"He is. I think he has it under control and I'm having second thoughts about tagging along."

Nic playfully placed a light hand on her forehead. "Are you feeling all right?"

Millie swatted at it. "Very funny. I don't want to get in the way."

There was a light rap on the door.

"Your date day surprise is here." Nic gave her a quick kiss and strode to the door. He returned with two of the ship's spa employees, along with maintenance crewmembers steering massage tables.

"What's this?"

"A couples' massage. I figured we could both use one." Nic led them outdoors. "With the recent expansion, we now have enough room out on our balcony for both tables."

With a little finagling, the men placed the tables far enough back to give them privacy, yet maintaining the sweeping views of the turquoise waters.

"You made sure the ship docked facing the water to give us more privacy," Millie said.

"Guilty as charged." Nic tilted his head, looking more than a little pleased with himself. "We have an amazing view."

"That we do."

While the massage therapists set up, Nic and Millie ran to the bedroom to swap out their work uniforms for spa robes.

"A massage sounds wonderful." Millie tightened her belt. "Thank you for such a special treat."

"The massage is only the first half," Nic said. "I have more."

"You're spoiling me rotten." Millie leaned in for a kiss.

"That's the plan. Forever if you'll let me."

They returned downstairs and found the spa employees playing catch with Scout.

Soft music played in the background as Millie settled onto the table. She closed her eyes and took a deep breath while the therapist began massaging her tight and taut muscles, starting at her neck and working her way down.

Millie must've dozed off because the next thing she knew, the woman was telling her they were done.

"I have to say, that was heavenly." Millie gripped the sheet and pivoted so her legs dangled over the side of the table. "I enjoyed every second."

"It was a wonderful massage," Nic chimed in as he draped the sheet around his lower half and slipped his robe back on. "I'll be right back."

"My pleasure, Captain Armati." The woman's cheeks turned a tinge of pink.

Millie's eyes narrowed, and she wondered if perhaps she should've kept a closer eye on Nic's masseuse.

He returned a short time later and handed each of them an envelope. "Thank you for meeting us here and taking time out of your busy day."

"You're welcome," Nic's gal, Kara, said as she handed him her card. "I would love to give you a massage again."

Millie saw them out and returned to find Nic folding the tables.

"Kara was very friendly."

"She did a good job, working all my sore muscles. I might ask for her next time."

"I'm sure she would love that," Millie said sarcastically. "I would love to give you a massage anytime," she mimicked the woman.

Nic laughed out loud. "C'mon Millie. She was working on the tip."

"She was working on something else," Millie muttered.

Nic snaked an arm around his wife's waist and pulled her close. "Have I ever told you how sexy you look when you get jealous?"

"No."

"Well, you do." Nic finished placing the massage tables outside the door and reached for his wife's hand. "Our early dinner won't be here for another hour. I was thinking we should hop in the shower and rinse off the massage oil."

"Now? Together?"

"You wash my back and I'll wash yours," he said in a husky voice.

Millie's heart flip-flopped. "This date day is getting better by the minute."

*****

Millie made a point of catching up with Sharky early the next morning. "Have you given Patterson the list of crewmembers who left the ship early in St. Kitts?"

"Yeah. We narrowed it down to three. I'm meeting them at nine. In about half an hour." Sharky slid his reading glasses on, propped his feet on the desk and cleared his throat. "Reef Savage."

"It wasn't Reef," Millie blurted out. "I'm surprised he's on the list."

"I said the same, but he still fits the MO. He was working the dock when we first arrived, has security clearance for the cargo area and access to the lost and found."

"Which means you also fit the criteria," Millie pointed out.

"That I do Millster, that I do. Maybe I did it."

"Did you?"

"Of course not," Sharky snapped. "Let's be serious, here."

"I am," Millie said. "Who are the other two?"

"Ross Farley and Carlos Valdez."

"Do you think either of them is capable of dealing drugs and possibly murdering someone?"

Sharky shrugged. "Anyone is capable of murder under the right circumstances."

"But in this case," Millie pressed.

"No, but then I like to think I'm an excellent judge of character and could pick out a criminal miles away."

"You mean like your ex-girlfriend, Svetlana Orlov, who kidnapped you and planned to kill you?"

"That was a low blow." Sharky playfully pressed his hand to his chest. "You really know how to hurt a guy."

"Sorry. I didn't mean to go there. But now you have Elvira and she doesn't strike me as the kidnapping / killer type." Millie patted Fin's head. "Do you want me to take Fin? I'm meeting up with Patterson. Danielle and I are assisting in the search."

Sharky hesitated. For some unknown reason, he was reluctant to let Fin out of his sight.

"I won't let him out of my sight," Millie promised. "He'll be fine."

"He's not used to being out of his element down here."

"I was the one who rescued him," she reminded him.

"True. Okay. I suppose if I'm gonna let anyone take Fin, it'll be you."

Before Sharky could change his mind, Millie scooped the cat up and headed toward the door. "We'll see you in a little while."

Sharky sprang from his chair and ran after her. "He doesn't like loud noises. Make sure you don't start banging around on stuff."

"We'll be fine," Millie called out as she hustled down the hall. She made a beeline for Patterson's office and found Oscar, Danielle, and Patterson already there.

"I see you have our helper," he said. "Sharky wasn't keen on handing him over."

"He couldn't refuse me since I was the one who rescued Fin." Millie placed the cat on the desk while Patterson went over the game plan.

At exactly nine, he got the text from Sharky telling him he was in a meeting.

"It's time to roll."

The group made the short trek to the crewmembers' quarters. Starting with Reef's cabin, Fin sniffed around while the others split up, searching the cramped space, careful to return everything to its original spot.

Fin finished first, after becoming disinterested in Reef's messy room. He stalked over to the door and waited for them to let him out.

"He doesn't mess around," Danielle said.

"No kidding," Oscar said. "Fin is ready to move on."

Up next was Ross Farley's room. Following the exact same steps, Millie carried Fin inside, except this time she felt him immediately stiffen. He let out a loud yowl.

Millie promptly set him on the floor, watching as the drug-sniffing cat approached the closet door and began pawing at it.

"He's onto something." Patterson eased the door open.

Fin disappeared inside and began yowling again.

"I need more light." Patterson opened the door as far as he could and began rummaging around inside. "Jackpot."

He emerged holding a black jacket with a St. Kitts and Nevis Patriots' emblem on the upper right-hand side.

Fin leapt into the air and swatted at the coat.

Patterson set it down, and the cat pounced on top, lightly pawing at the lining. "He's telling us there's something in the lining."

Using his pocketknife, he slit the seam and pulled out a small plastic baggie filled with white powder. "It appears we found Emilio's drug runner."

Fin finished sniffing around before returning to the jacket.

"Good boy." Millie patted his head. "Let's take a quick look around the last cabin."

"I'm going to give Sharky a call and ask him to send Ross over here."

With Patterson's permission, Millie and Danielle took Fin to Carlos Valdez's cabin three doors down.

The cat did a perimeter patrol and returned to the door, where Millie and Danielle stood waiting.

"Fin's giving us the all-clear." Millie reached into her pocket, pulled out some cat treats, and fed them to Fin. "We'll have to see what we can do about getting you a raise."

"Good kitty," Danielle said as she patted his head. "You saved me, big time. I'm going to buy you the biggest can of sardines I can find."

Fin purred loudly, butting his head against Danielle's hand.

The sound of voices echoed from the hallway.

"I think Ross is here." Millie scooped Fin up and held him close as she slipped out of Carlos's cabin and into the hallway where Patterson, Oscar, and a crewmember stood talking. The head of security held the Patriots' jacket in one hand and the packet of white powder in the other.

With a nod of Patterson's head, Oscar grabbed hold of the crewmember's arm, and they began escorting him down the hall.

Millie and Danielle shifted to the side to let them pass. Fin let out another loud yowl when he spotted the logoed jacket.

Ross shot Danielle a defiant look and hung his head as he was led away.

"You're off the hook." Millie patted her friend's arm. "And now Patterson can return the items that belonged to Casey."

Chapter 29

"Fin's gotta be the best drug-sniffing cat in the Caribbean." Sharky proudly patted the cat's head. "Aren't you buddy?"

"These are for him. It's a small token of my appreciation." Danielle set a stack of sardine cans on Sharky's desk. "You're the coolest cat ever."

"Ross admitted he conked Danielle on the head and tried to take the suitcase but swears up and down he had nothing to do with Emilio's death."

"In a nutshell," Millie said. "I'm sure you checked his schedule. Is there any chance he could have sneaked away to Brimstone Hill to meet Emilio?"

"It would have been hard, but not impossible," Sharky said. "I got to thinking about it. I would've noticed he was gone. Whether he contacted drug dealers after his shift ended? That's another story."

"Which means he didn't kill Emilio," Millie said. "Something tells me the St. Kitts' kingpin, Jiggy aka Jermaine Bilmow, was behind it. I think he found out Emilio was trying to invade his territory, confronted Emilio and then killed him."

"What we can confirm, according to Ross, is that Emilio moved to St. Kitts to start a drug operation, partnering with crewmembers from several ships, including cargo ships," Danielle said. "He set up a vendor booth at the port to use as a cover to run his operations with the help of crewmembers who had access to the cargo storage area."

"Ross claims he was supposed to grab the suitcase in Miami. He found Danielle was already there, freaked out and hit her on the head."

"And I showed up so he couldn't get the goods," Sharky said. "He knew the suitcase made it on board, figured out who Danielle was, seeing how he probably got a good look at her before whacking her and then started searching for it."

"I still don't get why Emilio involved me," Danielle said.

"Maybe the drugs were getting some attention or Emilio decided to cut Ross out and use you instead, knowing you would want your brother's belongings back," Millie theorized. "If this was the case, it was a dumb move on Emilio's part. He would've needed Ross's help for the next delivery."

"I have another theory," Danielle said. "Those drug dealers are a suspicious bunch. He could've suspected Ross planned to double-cross him and he needed that delivery. Either way, I'm glad it's over. I'm sad Emilio is dead, but also relieved."

"Because it means one less drug dealer is out on the streets," Millie guessed.

"And one less chance someone's brother gets sucked in," Danielle said. "Patterson is waiting for me in his office. He wants to return my brother's things. Thanks again, Sharky, for letting Fin help. If not for him, we might never have figured out what was going on."

"You got it. Me 'n Millie, we're partners." Sharky winked at Millie. "She knows she can call anytime and I've got her back."

"You're the best, Sharky. I owe you one."

"One?" he teased. "A lot more than just one."

"I'm sure you'll think of some way for me to pay you back." Millie followed Danielle out of Sharky's office. "Would you like me to go with you to pick up Casey's things?"

"Sure."

They climbed the stairs and walked to the other end of the corridor. When they got there, Millie waited in the hallway while Danielle went inside.

She emerged a short time later, carrying a small box. "This is it. I figured I would wait until later to find out exactly what Emilio sent."

"I don't blame you." Millie reached for her friend's arm. "Let's get some fresh air."

"I could use some." Danielle kept a tight grip on the box and its precious contents and followed Millie to the crew-only private outdoor area.

They headed in the opposite direction of a small group who sat at the bar and stopped when they reached the railing.

"Red sky at night, sailor's delight," Millie quipped.

"It's beautiful." Danielle sighed. "Casey would've loved all of this. The excitement. The travel. Being on the go all the time. He was so young and full of life. It's such a shame."

"It is."

They grew quiet, contemplating their voyage. It had been a doozy. Mervin. Emilio. Brimstone Hill.

Danielle ran a light hand over the top of the box. "At least I got Casey's stuff back. Having it means a lot."

"I know it does."

Her lower lip quivered as she stared out into the open waters. "He almost made it. He was almost there. If only…"

Millie placed an arm around her shoulders. "No more looking in the rearview mirror, torturing yourself with the what ifs. Focus on the memories, when you visited Lake Mirror, the happy times when you were together."

"You're right." Danielle lifted the box. "This ripped the wound open, and it hurts all over again."

"You did your best, tried your hardest and loved him until the end. He knew that. You need to forgive yourself."

"I…will." Danielle sucked in a breath. "Casey's favorite saying was, 'In the end, our only regrets are the chances we didn't take and the decisions we waited too long to make.'"

"And he was right." Millie leaned in and hugged her. "Words to live by, my friend. Words to live by."

The end.

The Series Continues!

More Cruise Director Millie books coming soon!

Dear Reader,

I hope you enjoyed reading "Christmas Cruise Crisis." Would you please take a moment to leave a review? It would mean so much. Thank you!

–Hope Callaghan

Join The Fun!

Get Updates On New Releases, FREE and Discounted Books, Giveaways, & More!

hopecallaghan.com

Read More by Hope

Millie's Cruise Ship Cozy Mystery Series

Hoping for a fresh start after her recent divorce, sixty something Millie Sanders, lands her dream job as the assistant cruise director onboard the "Siren of the Seas." Too bad no one told her murder is on the itinerary.

Garden Girls Cozy Mystery Series

A lonely widow finds new purpose for her life when she and her senior friends help solve a murder in their small Midwestern town.

Garden Girls - The Golden Years

The brand new spin-off series of the Garden Girls Mystery series! You'll enjoy the same fun-loving characters as they solve mysteries in the cozy town of Belhaven. Each book will focus on one of the Garden Girls as they enter their "golden years."

Lack of Luxury Series (Liz and the Garden Girls)

Green Acres meets the Golden Girls in this brand new cozy mystery spin-off series featuring Liz and the Garden Girls!

Made in Savannah Cozy Mystery Series

After the mysterious death of her mafia "made man" husband, Carlita Garlucci makes a shocking discovery. Follow the Garlucci family saga as Carlita and her daughter try to escape their NY mob ties and make a fresh start in Savannah, Georgia. They soon realize you can run but can't hide from your past.

Divine Cozy Mystery Series

After relocating to the tiny town of Divine, Kansas, strange and mysterious things begin to happen to businesswoman, Jo Pepperdine and those around her.

Easton Island Mystery Series

Easton Island - Looking Glass Cottage is the continuing saga of one woman's journey from incredible loss to finding a past she knew nothing about, including a family who both embraces and fears her and a charming island that draws her in. This inspirational series is for lovers of family sagas, mystery, and a touch of romance.

Samantha Rite Mystery Series

Heartbroken after her recent divorce, a single mother is persuaded to book a cruise and soon finds herself caught in the middle of a deadly adventure. Will she make it out alive?

Sweet Southern Sleuths Short Stories Series

Twin sisters with completely opposite personalities become amateur sleuths when a dead body is discovered in their recently inherited home in Misery, Mississippi.

Meet Hope Callaghan

Hope Callaghan is an American mystery author who loves to write clean, fun-filled women sleuth cozy mysteries with a touch of faith and romance. She is the author of more than 90 novels in nine different series.

Born and raised in a small town in West Michigan, she now lives in Florida with her husband. She is the proud mother of 3 wonderful children.

When she's not doing the thing she loves best - writing mysteries - she enjoys cooking, traveling and reading books.

Get a free cozy mystery book, new release alerts, and giveaways at hopecallaghan.com

Divine Dark Chocolate Peanut Butter Brownie Recipe

Ingredients:

1 - 18 oz pkg. brownie mix

1-3/4 cups peanut butter chips (10 oz.)

1 - 14-oz. can sweetened condensed milk

1/2 cup creamy peanut butter

1 teaspoon vanilla extract

1-3/4 cups dark chocolate chips (10 oz.)

3/4 cup heavy cream

1/2 cup chopped walnuts or peanuts

Directions:

-Preheat oven to 350°F.

-Spray a 13- x 9-inch baking dish with coconut oil or cooking spray.

- Prepare brownie mix according to package directions.

-Pour batter into greased baking dish.

-Bake as directed or until a wooden toothpick

comes out clean.

-Remove from oven. Cool completely.

While the brownies are cooling:

-Place peanut butter chips, sweetened condensed milk, peanut butter, vanilla, and salt in a medium microwavable bowl.

-Microwave on HIGH 1 minute.

-Remove and stir.

-Spoon evenly over cooled brownies.

-Place dark chocolate chips and heavy cream in a small microwavable bowl.

-Microwave on HIGH 30 seconds.

-Remove and stir.

-Microwave another 30 seconds.

-Repeat until chocolate has melted.

-Pour melted chocolate over peanut butter mixture on brownies.

-Refrigerate brownies until top chocolate layer is firm, about 1 hour.

-Sprinkle top with walnuts or peanuts.

-Slice into 32 bars and serve.

Printed in Great Britain
by Amazon